Preface

It was a brisk, cool day in Miami, Florida. Alabama had just won its' 15th National Championship game. Nick Saban approached the microphone for his winning speech. With all the enthusiasm that Coach Saban brings, he began to speak. "I never read Bamagirlluvsu, but most of the football players did. We attribute our success together as a team to her courage, ambition, and drive. We would not be here today had it not been for her inspiring words."

Okay. Okay. So it is a dream. Just like I can dream that Oprah calls me for her book club. That is what life is all about. Our dreams. Our goals. It is up to each of us to make it happen. With the help and strength of family and friends, and the encouragement behind the love that they have for us, we can achieve anything. We keep moving forward to be the best that we can be.

I want to thank all of my friends and family for their continued love and support daily. This book would not have been possible without all of you. I also want to thank my ex-husbands for all that you did. Without you guys, Bamagirlluvsu would not have evolved. (Smiling)

I also wish to thank all of the "fish." Each of you was a pleasure to meet, in your own distinct way. If you find that a story in this book resembles a small piece of your life, then perhaps that story is about you. If you find further that the story is embellished (or unembellished), just smile to yourself, knowing that you know the truth.

To those of you that I "blew off" I apologize sincerely. Please don't take it personally. Just because Bamagirlluvsu wasn't attracted to you doesn't mean that you aren't attractive to someone. After all, there are a "million fish in the sea." Don't give up. "Just keep swimming..."

Thank You.
Sandy Gowers

A very special thank you to my Familyman333. Without you (and without the angels and the help from God), this book would not have been possible. Happy Birthday! And many, many more birthdays to come. "I simply pray for a lifetime of todays!" I love you.

A special thanks to the "brains" behind the internet and social networking sites for providing the means and the opportunity to pursue new friendships.

To the musicians, singers, and songwriters, a special appreciation for the contribution that your hard work makes to our lives daily. There is always a song that can be applied to the unique circumstances in our lives. Thank you for the songs behind the "Song Applications."

Prologue

Roll Tide! I felt I should get that one out of the way before I begin. I promise to reference that only once or twice... but what would a book titled "Bamagirlluvsu" be without at least one good Roll Tide!?

Who am I and what am I doing? I am a 49 year old (I mean young) single lady from the south, a southern girl, raised by a single parent. I was born a poor girl with little religious affiliation; parents divorcing when I was age six. Mom was pregnant with my younger sister at the time. I have a twin brother and an older sister that really took care of all of us. Mom passed away of cancer when I was 18 years old and dad died five years later of a massive heart attack. Having been an alcoholic his entire life, it was surprising that he was with us as long as he was.

I have been married three times....well four (if you count the fact that I married my first husband twice). And I guess it must be counted. Know this about my relationships and I must make it perfectly clear. It is not me! LOL. That is what we choose to say. And we all believe it. There is the old saying: there are three sides to every story: his side, her side, and the truth. The truth is this...my side is the truth....still smiling...still writing...

Being old and in love is just like being young and in love. Getting the chills from head to toe...waiting on that phone call (uhhhhh....or in this generation....), that text, email, picture, Facebook© or Twitter© post! Just waiting.... hoping.... PRAYING.... to hear something. Yes. We have all been there. Whether at the age of 13, 21, 35, 49 (awwwww – almost 50), rejection still hurts. Attention is still warranted and sometimes granted. Sometimes not!

Who am I and what am I doing? I am single again. AGAIN! For the ugghhhh FOURTH time! Dang! I have been divorced for two years and it has been an incredible learning experience. I have met men of all sizes, shapes, and class types. Can you believe there are men OUR age that still don't know what it is to acquire and maintain a job? Wow! I am sure there are women like this too. Those online searching for the man of their dreams....only their dreams are filled with dollar signs. Not me! I have dated the poorest of the poor and the richest of the rich. And each and every experience has given me a new-found outlook on life.

Who are WE and what are WE doing? We are all human beings. Searching. Looking. Longing. Wanting that special someone that can truly be our soul mate! Longing for that sensuous kiss....you know the one! Where the hot, sexy man takes you and with a gentle force pushes you against the wall and gives you every ounce of his being. You stop briefly. Weak in the knees. You can't breathe and don't care if you do or not. Yes, that kiss that literally takes your breath away!

So here we are. The baby boomers - those of us born between the years 1946 and 1964. Baby boomers have been known to be associated with rejection. Really? Rejection. Not us. There are over 75 million of us in the world today. What does that tell you? Our parents had a really good time having babies, during a time of war as the men were leaving to go away to fight for their country. The wives were left behind pregnant, waiting for the return of the dads. Many who never returned due to death or abandonment. So should we feel this rejection?

In my case, feelings of rejection are derived from a father who was an alcoholic and was never around. Then when he decided to be around, discovered that his daughters were of the female persuasion and didn't distinguish the fact that they were his blood. Rejection brought on by having a father who sexually molested his "girls" and then denied it when it was brought to the forefront of it all. Two daughters at the ages of 12 and 18 were forced to sweep it under the rug and pretend it never happened. So, yes, a rejection by the male population brought on by a new, unethical appreciation of a father to his daughters. This made me a person of heart; of forgiveness. I can forgive everything that anyone could ever do to me. After all, if my own father, the male figure in my life that should have been my hero, can strip me of every ounce of dignity that I could possess, and still expect unconditional love and forgiveness, then why shouldn't every other man in my life? And why shouldn't this become an easy, effortless thing for me to do?

So that is my heart. Open. Caring. Affectionate. Easy. Longing. Needing. Wanting. Searching. Anticipating.....

Revealing this side of me isn't easy. But it is necessary for you to know who I am. It is necessary to help you understand my personality. It is our past that has made us who we are in the present. I am not spilling my guts about this terrible heart-breaking time in my life to acquire empathy, sympathy, or sorrow. I want you to laugh. I want you to smile. I laugh. I smile. Nothing or no-one can ever bring me down and keep me there! I am strong! In this world that can sometimes sink the ship, this ship will always stay afloat. No. I am more than that. I am more than floating. I sail! I rise above it all and keep on living! I keep loving and giving with all that I have. This is how we don't let our hearts become bitter. It is the ability to keep our hearts open for love. It is the fact that we could choose to drown, but instead we pull our head up out of the water, a little at a time, until we can breathe again.

Song Application - "If what doesn't kill you makes you stronger..." - Kelly Clarkson ©

Songs are a very big part of who I am. I love music. I can be having a conversation with anyone and that conversation triggers a song in my head and I just sing a line. "Song application of the day" I will say. I shouldn't say "of the day" because there are generally at least five, six, ten, or twenty per day. I love it! My kids will say, "Mom has a song for everything." And I do. I will be dispersing a few of these throughout the book, as a signatory of who I am and the songs that touch my heart and life daily.

So here we are. The baby boomers. Ages 48 – 66. Some of us (not me of course – I have already shared who I am). But…a lot of us have been married our entire life, in love in the beginning with the most beautiful man or woman we had ever met. We had all of those sensual desires and laughter, along with a common ground with our mate. And we were there for a lifetime. We experienced all of our "firsts" with this person: our first kiss, our first sexual experience, our first home, the first child, and our first "real" job. We grew closer to this person than anyone could ever be to a person. This was the man/woman we should/would spend the rest of our life with. The children grew up. The job got complacent. The sex got …less and less…to NONE. The passion for life and love was gone. Or was it just hidden, deep within our souls, begging to get out!?

The blessed ones. Those who knew that this is truly a commitment and believed in "till death do you part." The blessed ones were able to work through this. Perhaps get counseling or perhaps through their love and faith in God. This blessed, and minority group of people, remain happily married and get to experience something that I never will see: growing old with someone that you have a deep-rooted past with. You can have shared holidays. Share the children and grandchildren. And you can take care of each other as you face the inevitable crossing to the other side.

I have shared with my children this life-learning lesson multiple times. There isn't a single day that goes by that I don't regret the mistakes made during my first marriage. There isn't a single day that I don't wish things could have worked out. God really knew what he was doing when he said, "till death do you part." Children suffer. Hearts are broken. Divorce is hard. Would I go back if I could? No. Absolutely not! What is done is done! You can't change the past. And without the mistakes made, my beautiful daughter would not be in this world, giving me the pleasure of her love daily.

So, there are those of us who are out here in this single world again….with that feeling of rejection overcoming us and facing a new world. And it is a world far different from the one that we were in when we were in our early adult years. Remember those days? No cell phones. No gaming systems. The internet? What's that? If you wanted to stay in touch with someone, you did so by "snail mail." This could take seven to ten days just to send a hand-written letter to your new friends.

Remember when you would meet someone and they would ask you out, they would come to your house to pick you up and would have to meet your parents first? Ask permission to go out with you? Show honor and respect for you in order to win your heart? Remember the nights of talking on the phone until 2 a.m. in the morning, longing to see this person again. Getting caught by your parents and told, "GET OFF THAT PHONE! IT'S PAST TEN OCLOCK! NO-ONE SHOULD BE ON THE PHONE THIS LATE! GO TO BED!"

Today, the younger generation has a cell phone at the age of eight years. Wow! Does an eight-year old really need a cell phone? With the era of increasing divorces, the cell phone provides a means for the "other parent" to stay in contact with their child. And the internet! Wow! What a concept! This continuous connectivity of computers, cell-phones, I-pads, and gaming systems has created a whole new world of networking.

Social networking. Children go away to camp and return with new "Facebook friends©" that they can communicate with daily with no time delay like we had with "snail mail."

And we baby boomers. We have joined them! We are a new, older, technologically advanced generation. We are bigger and better (I am not so sure about this one), and we are able to join in the ranks of online dating! A new way to meet people. A way that you can be whatever and whomever you want to be. But be careful! False advertisers do get caught! If one is truly online to meet the "love of their life" then telling the truth is of the utmost importance.

However, there are those that have been rejected. They believe they have nothing to offer. So they create a better version of who they are. They lie! Plain and simple. They lie! Those of us, who have become more advanced in our on-line dating skills, have learned how to pick these guys out! We can find them. Reject them. Reject them some more! And finally, block them! Great is the computer age!

The idea of this book actually came to me from one of my dates. I mentioned writing a book for my profession (accounting – ughh. That would have to be boring). And this date (I will reveal him later)…said to me over drinks: "Am I part of the research?" "Huh?" I asked. "Research for your book? The one on online dating?" I responded, "I am not writing a book on on-line dating!"….AND THEN THE LIGHTBULB WENT OFF! "I am not writing a book on on-line dating. But I could! I have some stories to tell! What a great idea!"

So here I am. Ready. Willing. And desiring to tell my experiences. This has been fun. Entertaining. Self-indulging. And addictive. I have a 2011 red camaro (birthday present to me from me after my divorce – to prove to myself that I was deserving of better – as if I needed to prove that to myself). I commute daily 70 miles to my job. Travel time – one hour and fifteen minutes one way. I decided when creating my profile, that if I am willing to commute 70 miles for my job, then why not to meet the love of my life!? So I set my profile distance to 100 miles. I live in Northwest Alabama (do I dare throw in another Roll Tide now? – Nah! I will wait). Listing 100 miles as my criteria, this gets me Memphis, Birmingham, Nashville, and Huntsville (which is where I work). A lot of bigger cities. Well, bigger than small-town Alabama. A way that I can meet more professional, more distinguished men. Men who have a life. Men who have a story to tell. We all have one. And they are all different. But we are all here, in this cyber dating world, for a reason and we are searching for something…for someone to complete us.

Song Application - "I Am So Much Cooler Online" – Brad Paisley ©

My story will be a "brutally honest and entertaining" one. It must be. Life is too short to focus on anything other than the entertaining aspect of these life experiences. Oh yes, of course, I could focus on the degradation that occurred from some of my dates. I could focus inward to the hurt and self-destruction that may have resulted from putting my heart on the line so many times, to be rejected yet still again and again. I could focus on that, but why? Why should I bring up this negative aspect, when I have learned so much from these experiences that have turned this period of my life into a very positive and uplifting time. I have grown into a more self-confident woman of the world. I can get into my red camaro and drive anywhere I want to drive and meet anyone I want to meet. And…they WANT to meet me!

Each of these dates was brought to me for a reason. Sometimes, that reason may not be about me (although, sometimes I want the world to be about me). Sometimes, my new association with others allowed me to be in their lives at a time when they needed someone. I became the person that allowed them to grow, or achieve a new self-respect. These experiences were never all about me!

As I reveal the different people I have met, and the areas in which they have touched my heart and my life, you will find that I am a better person. My expectation of others is not as grand as it used to be. Wow! Can you believe that is a negative? That maybe my expectations should remain high? The problem is that I had grown so self-indulgent that I believed everyone should think the way that I did. If someone didn't see things my way, because after all, the way that I viewed life was the right way. If someone failed to see my viewpoint, then I no longer needed them in my life.

I always had the ability to see the big picture in things. Beyond the day to day. An insight into the extended version of what was happening. I didn't see just what was right in front of me. I could see things beyond that. Consequences. Rewards. I had my own internal crystal ball.

That is why I could sit before you and know that my version of the truth, my viewpoint, was the correct and only one. This cost a lot of friends during my life. I couldn't get close to people because they didn't wear their feelings on their sleeve. They couldn't see beyond what lie in front of them. So they didn't know what I knew. Because they were slighted in their thinking, they were wrong. They did not have my insight. How could I remain friends with those individuals that did not do right by others? They could use those around them and not even know they were using them. But I knew what others didn't know. So I could walk. And I walked away often.

My new dating experiences allowed me to open up this small-town Alabama heart and mind to a new realization that people are different and it is okay. These experiences allowed me to become more versatile in my thoughts and knowledge. I was able to branch out of small town mentality and venture into a world that I did not know existed. I was not afraid. I was nervous at times, but never afraid.

I want my story to be real. I want to convey the ideas of cyber dating / on-line dating, and social networking to others so that they may realize the world is bigger than just the few familiar streets that they drive down daily. Many times, we settle for love. We believe that we don't have the opportunity to meet our soul mate or that he doesn't exist. We grow up in our hometowns, with our neighbors and friends. Everyone knows everyone. And they make it their business to know everything. We begin to mold ourselves into what is expected of us to become.

If we had opportunity to be ourselves, where we weren't being judged by others, do you think we would all take that chance? Of course, we would. If we could branch out of our daily lives into a new person and have excitement in our lives where no-one ever knew what we did or thought, we would all jump in our cars and drive cross country to be the person that we were never allowed to be.

But why weren't we allowed to be ourselves? To be more than just what was expected? Because life happened. Life came along. WE fell in love. WE got married. WE had children. WE fell into routine, complacent jobs. And WE became what life made us become. I had a chance, through the invention of the internet and online networking, to meet new people, explore my inner self, and to become ME!

I want my story to be honest, as honest as it can be. I will tell of my adventures. And I will tell them with the vigor and passion of which they were experienced. I will reveal a side of me that those in my small town can't wait to tell their neighbor. I may become the gossip of the town. Oh no! I may become the outcast! Honestly, after four divorces, I am probably already talked about. So, let's give them something else to talk about.

Song Application – "Let's Give'em Something to Talk About" – Bonnie Raitt©

I am prefacing in this paragraph, that some of my stories will be "somewhat little white lies." Yes, some of the stories will be embellished and some will be unembellished (is that a word) to protect the innocent and the guilty. I will also change the screen names and locations of my dates. I want to maintain discretion for them. They deserve to have their lives remain private. The purpose of this book is not to implicate anyone.

This book is not about sex. We can all find that any night of the week at the local bar. If you want to read about fantasy sex, read the amazing book, Fifty Shades of Grey© and its sequels. The purpose of this story is to reveal the fun I have had and the lessons I have learned. It is about the heart… reality… feelings… discoveries made through adventures taken. Enjoy!

Life is so much more than sitting at home on the couch and watching television or playing video games. Life is so much more than chatting on Facebook© or POF© or other sights. Make those initial connections! Then…. Get out! Take a road trip! You never know what adventures you will encounter, or what new life's experiences that you may have that otherwise would only remain a dream. Take an opportunity to explore the person that YOU are! Life is too short! DANCE!

♥♥Bamagirlluvsu♥♥

Divorce sucks. Yes. I said it. Divorce sucks. Actually, I am happier than I have ever been. I would rather have no-one in my life than to have a bad relationship. And my relationships were bad, with infidelity, anger, hostility and the destruction of family. I am at peace now. I can come home and retreat to my "woman cave" and be happy to be there. No worries. I don't have to wonder which man I am coming home to today. Is it Dr. Jekyll or Mr. Hyde? There is no-one. And I am okay with that. Because the "woman cave" is my refuge, my happy place.

NOT!

Yes! Yes! I am happy! I am! Really! I have Facebook©. I have now reconnected with old high school friends. Friends that remind me of the person I used to be….no….the person that I still am. I am chatting nightly with these old friends. And they tell me about me. They tell me how I used to laugh. How happy I was. How my laughter would ring through the hallways at the school. "Your laugh is contagious," they would say. So yes, I am happy. Because I am free to be me again. I am free to laugh again.

Meeting someone new is the farthest thing from my mind. Or is it? I want companionship. I have spent my entire life searching for that special man, the man who loves unconditionally and unselfishly. Why can't I find him? Why is it so hard for someone to love me the way that I want and need to be loved? I know how it should be. I know how it MUST be! If I can't have it that way, then I won't have it at all.

So why did I stay in my previous relationship as long as I did? It wasn't right. Yet I stayed. For five years I lived in a very unhealthy relationship. There was so much anger and hurt in my home. And my children! What was I thinking? Did what my father do really leave me believing that I deserved no more than that? That any man in my life could treat me with dishonor and disrespect and I should just accept it? That I should just look at him and smile because after all, it is who I am. It is what I was taught. It is what I do. I forgive. I forget. I just get over it! Over and over.

Did I really believe that I could hide in the closet many nights with a Bible in hand praying? "God, I know I made you a promise. I know that I made myself a promise. I would not leave this marriage. This is it for me. I AM COMMITTED! I AM! Nothing you can throw at me will ever make me break my promise, neither to myself nor to you."

My forgiving and forgetful heart gave me the strength and courage to remain in this relationship for over five years. I waited and prayed for a sign from God to tell me that it was okay to leave. Each and every sign that came before me, I questioned. "Is this a sign that God has given me his permission to walk away or is it a test of my promise?" I had a constant battle between my heart and my mind. Finally, God gave me the final sign. And the decision was revealed to me. So, I am divorced. There is no man in my life, but I am not alone.

This book isn't supposed to be about the negativity in my life. It isn't supposed to be about the actions of an alcoholic father. It isn't supposed to be about the fact that I married my father (funny how we seem to do that). This book is supposed to be frolic in nature; uplifting; happy. Because that is who I am. At least now. Now that I am free to be me. AGAIN. I return to the happy, smiling girl with the contagious laugh. Yes. This book is not about my father issues (though it could be). We all have a story to tell. We all have the life we lived that brought us to where we are today. After all, we are all by-products of our environment. Every road we have taken has led us here.

Song Application - "God Bless the Broken Road" – Rascal Flatts©

So here we are, facing an opportunity that we have never faced before. Do we settle for being alone? Are we happy being alone? Many of us will tell ourselves that we don't want another man (or woman) in our life. After all, wasn't the life we had before miserable? Aren't we happy to be out of prison now? Aren't we glad to be free again? Aren't we glad to have our "woman cave" or our "man cave" that we can call our own? That we can come home to each and every day without worry of what or "who" we are coming home to that day. Aren't we happy to find peace? YES!

AGAIN!!!!! NO!!!!

There is something in each of us that longs for a connection. We long to have that feeling of care and love that we never had. Recall the rejection associated with baby boomers. Well maybe, just maybe, we are tired of rejection. We want acceptance. After all, we are human. We were brought into this world, a simple naked bundle of joy, longing to be held. And we were held continuously. We got hungry, we cried. We got wet, we cried. Someone would hold us, cuddle with us, or snuggle with us. Close. Empathizing. Taking the pain away. We grew up with caring, loving parents. Or sometimes we did not. But either way, we were left longing for the continued love and affection, or left longing for what we never had. It is inevitable. WE WANT TO BE LOVED! WE WANT TO BE TOUCHED! WE WANT TO BE CARESSED!

So my story continues. I am divorced again. Still longing. Still searching. Still wanting that special someone in my life. And I am not going to give up until I find him. I know that he is out there in this vast world. After all, there are 75 million baby boomers. One of them has to be for me! At least one of them has to be able to recognize that I have a heart and I am willing to share it unconditionally with him. FOREVER!

So here I go, laptop in front of me in my "woman cave" all safe and secure. And I bring up my first on-line dating sight. I don't know what I am doing. But I am going to give it a try. And I am going to pay for this thing. After all, I can go out on a Friday night and blow a good fifty bucks having fun with friends. Why shouldn't I be willing to invest a little money in my love life? So I begin.

I complete the questionnaire. The simple things. Name. Date of birth. Married. Divorced. Do you have kids? Do you want kids? etc. The simple things that we can answer about ourselves. The next section, where you have to describe yourself and what you are looking for in this big cyber world, is much more difficult.

Mmmmmmmm. I ponder. I guess I am looking for what everyone else is looking for out here. So that is what I write. "I am looking for what everyone else is looking for. We are all out here for a reason, to find true love." Wow! Short and sweet. Not much to say. What else can I say? So I stop. I submit my profile. And I upload pictures. What picture should be my main profile picture? "I know." I think to myself. "The picture of me lying on the bed in Las Vegas last summer. My Female Soul Mate (You will learn about my FSM's in a later chapter) took the picture just before we went out to see Phantom of the Opera. That is a great picture! Yes, it should grab a lot of eyes!" So I upload it. And I wait. And I wait….

The search got interesting. The responses were varied. I got addicted to this feeling and I got addicted fast. I have met a lot of interesting men. I have made a lot of new friends. I have made some enemies that were "blocked" and sent to cyber space never to be seen or heard from again. Wow, don't we wish it were really that easy in life?

I learned that rejection doesn't hurt so badly online. People reject you and it is okay, because there is one more profile after that one. There are so many potential dates sitting right at your fingertips, the fact that one (or two, or ten, or twenty, or even one hundred) rejects you, just opens the opportunity for you to meet one more person. It's simple. It's easy. Online-shopping is addictive!

Then.....my profile was blocked! Shut down! I couldn't get into the website at all. Why? I hadn't forgotten my password. My God, I had logged in every night for a month. How could I forget my password? So I called customer service regarding my inability to access the site. I was in panic mode. Someone might be trying to reach me. I could miss out on the love of my life! LOL. The operator on the other end of the line proceeded to tell me, "We have detected suspicious activity with your account and we had to shut you down. You can create a new account under a different email address and a different method of payment, but you can no longer use your old account." My first account was created under the name "sandyinbama." "Sandyinbama" could no longer exist. But I loved the "bama" reference. I wanted to use that. After all, that is what I am. An Alabama Girl.

And there it was! My name. "Maybe," I thought. "Just maybe no one has used it." So I go to the computer and I proceed with "Bamagirlluvsu." Perfect. The name was perfect. And no one else had thought to use it. Thus, I was born. Or cyber-me was re-born under the name "Bamagirlluvsu." And I continued with my online shopping.

One week later. Shut down again. AGAIN! How! Why? What is happening with my profile? Forget this! I am finished! I am not doing this again! Of course, I was given a full refund and a free month each time my service was interrupted. But who wants this? And now, I am getting emails on my personal email from women in Russia who have seen my profile and WANT me. Who stole my profile and just what are they doing with it? I replied back to the emails, "Please, tell me where you saw my information. I am not seeking a female. I am only looking for the male gender!" Wow! No-one would answer me back! "This is fishy," I thought. "Really fishy." Then I remembered. There was another website and it doesn't cost anything. "Plenty of Fish." POF.com©. I will give it a shot!

So now I am in the world of fishing. "Just keep swimming. Just keep swimming." (From the movie "Finding Nemo")©. I am a little fish out here in the big ocean trying to find my way. And I am fishing under the screen name "Bamagirlluvsu." No way could "Bamagirlluvsu" die. I am alive and swimming, trying to find the ONE fish that is waiting for me. He is out here in this great big blue sea and I will find him.

So…I login:

My profile "catch phrase" – "To live is to love, to love is to live" comes from a poem that I wrote when I was a young teenager. The poem was from a young girl's heart.

To live is to love; to love is to live.
 I live to love, but I love to live.
To live is to be what you want to be;
To see the things that you want to see;
To do the things that you want to do;
And that's why I'm in love with you.
To live is to go where you want to go;
To know the things that you want to know;
To say the things you know are true;
And that's why I'm in love with you.
To live is to love; to love is to live.
LIVE TO LOVE AND YOU WILL LOVE TO LIVE!"©

Wow, as I sit here and recite the poem from so long ago, I am reminded of the naivety of a young girl's heart. The innocence of not knowing the hurt in this world. The openness to love and what it can bring. As I decipher the real meaning of the words, I realize that when I wrote them, they meant something so different than what they mean to me today. At the innocent age of twelve, I had so much faith and hope for the future. Yes, I had been raised in a broken home, without the nurturing mother, and with a father who was never around. But, I KNEW my life would be different. I knew that all men were born inherently good and would be guided to do right by others. That meant that somewhere out there, there was someone for me. Someone that I could be myself with and never worry about any consequences. The entire meaning of the poem was that you can live life with love in your heart, but if you lose yourself in the process, then you haven't gained real love at all.

That is the real meaning behind the words. But, at the time that I allowed those words to flow from my head to my hand and then to the paper in front of me, I simply had an overflowing faith and hope for the future. My life would be much better than that of which I had watched my mother live. So, I sit before my laptop and my catch phrase becomes "To live is to love, to love is to live," because I want those potential male partners to know that I am about being yourself with whomever you are with. I will live my life to the fullest and love with everything in me. Living and loving with all I can. I am happy and content.

Uploading pictures was fun. I wanted various pictures that illustrated a little about all sides of me. So, I uploaded a picture with my daughter because I am a Mom, first and foremost. I wanted a picture with one of my best friends, to show I know how to have fun. I had to put a picture with my new red, hot camaro (not because I am materialistic – but because this car signifies that I deserved better, and that I am at a better place in my life). I also wanted the sexual, sensual pictures. Because that is a big part of who I am. I love to feel sexy. I love dressing in a manner in which accentuates my better attributes. After all, most all women hate their bodies. Therefore, we must dress so that our clothing compliments the better parts. And that picture that I made in Vegas on the bed, it had to stay. I don't care what anyone says....I looked hot in that picture.

The profile:

I am seeking a man – DUH! To whoever stole my profile….I don't want a woman!

Needs Test: I don't have a clue….I don't "NEED" anything….I <u>WANT</u>. So, I skip it!

Do you drink? Socially, of course. Most everyone that drinks will answer this way. Get real people, do you really think someone will answer they are an alcoholic here!?

Marital Status: (Ok, yes there are some married people out here fishing). I AM DIVORCED. AND I AM SINGLE!

Pets: None and I do not want any. LOL. They don't have a social security number and I can't get a tax deduction for them. I am away from home too much to care for them. And I can barely feed myself and my three children!

Profession: Accountant (What else do I say here? I wish I could say more. I am not your stereotypical accountant! I can let my hair down and have fun! I am not a prune)!

Do you have a car? Seriously? Really? Do you have people answer this one no? I mean, surely there is no-one under the age of 16 on a dating website? Who thinks of these questions?

For: Long Term (Other choices: dating…. mmmmm ….seeking intimate encounters…. Do people really answer this one? Mmmmmm).

Chemistry: (View her chemistry results). Yes, I took the test. This tells no-one anything. Anyone can fit into these molds just by answering the questions the right or wrong way. Enough said.

Do you want children: Yes/No/Maybe .... mmmmm...
I said NO. I mean, I already have three of my own. I don't
care if you have children, I just don't want any more. I guess
this question is needed and necessary.

Do you do drugs? (Define drugs please). What are
drugs? Prescriptions? Marijuana? Cocaine? Mmmmmmm?
Can someone please define drugs? I mean, for me this is not a
hard question. I do not do drugs. But others seem to have
difficulty distingquishing between the word "no" and exactly
what is a drug. Some questions are just hard to answer, I
guess.

Eye Color: (Who freakin cares?) Really. If someone's
eye color is a deal breaker for you, then you are just so out of
luck in this world of dating. Because, eye color would be the
least of your worries. Again, who writes this stuff?

Do you have children? (Really important question.
Seriously...no sarcasm here). If you have children, would you
consider a man who had none? I am thinking the man has to
have fathered at least one of those little rascals in his lifetime to
understand the bond between a parent and a child. How can a
man understand the needs and wants of a child, if they never
had any? AGAIN! VERY IMPORTANT!

Longest Relationship: (I guess this could matter). I
mean if you are pursuing a man in his late 40's to early 50's
and his longest relationship is 6 months or one year, I would
think you could recognize a sure-fire sign right off that this
man has some sort of commitment issues. Or women just hate
him! Either way, something is definitely wrong!

That was the easy part. The yes or no questions. The
simple answers about who you are and what others may
perceive as deal breakers. So that part is finished. The next
part of the profile was something just as easy. List some of

your interests. Things you like to do that will allow others to see if you may have something in common. Hobbies.

I stop. I think. Wow, I don't do anything! I have spent my entire life trying to please whatever man was in my life, so I assumed his hobbies, his interests. So how can I decide right now…right this second…what I like to do? Maybe this is what my sister meant when she said to me, "Sandy, take time out for you. Enjoy yourself. Find out what you like to do before you date. You need a period of self-discovery!" Obviously, I did not listen. I had my own ideas to finding myself.

I continued on with my thoughts. Okay. So what do I like to do? My daughter. My sons. The most important part of my life. So yes, I must start with that… "Watching my daughter play sports." My boys are older now, living their own lives. So, I don't mention them here. What else? Something else. Okay. I like to go to the beach (from what I have seen on these sights, you can connect with anyone with this commonality). Alabama football. Roll Tide. (Wow did I just get in another Roll Tide)?

I love going to my local bar. My Cheers. So I include that. It is another safe haven. I have met a lot of friends that I can just hang out with and be comfortable, including the DJ and his wife. Everyone always makes me feel right at home. I formed a relationship with the people here in which I could share my life's stories and we would all laugh. Laughter was prevalent and we all need that in our lives.

On any night you can walk into that bar and hear me bellowing out a song, or hear my laughter above everyone else, and you may see me attempting a little dance, like the "wobble." As my daughter would say, "scared of dat!" I love this place. It is only a few miles from my home. After going into the bar a few times, it wasn't long until everyone there knew me. Yes, a cliché, but everyone really does know my name.

I haven't bowled in a while, but I loved it when I did. So I added that as well. I needed to list something else. I didn't want to look like I had no life at all. Really, all I did was go to work, come home, and take care of children. Watch my daughter play sports (that one is real). Go to my Cheers, sing and dance. Have a few margaritas. Come home. And do it all over the next day. Yes, I had a boring life. A boring, PEACEFUL life. My profile must show more than that. After all, I AM NOT YOUR STEREOTYPICAL ACCOUNTANT!

The "about me" section was next. This is the most difficult part of the profile. Telling people about who you are. Remember, we are a rejected generation. But we want the world to believe otherwise. We want to portray that we haven't lived through drama in our lives. And that we haven't spent the last years of our lives "wading to x-hell." You don't want anyone to know there is "baby daddy" drama or any "ex"drama whatsoever. After all, you are on-line for a purpose. You are here to sell yourself. So this has to be good. No, this must be great! It must display confidence. And it must tell people who you are, what you stand for and what you represent. This profile must be an illustration of what you have to offer and, just like your pictures, must portray a little about all sides of you. So here goes:

About Me

Love is like the game of golf.

Sometimes, you get a bogie.

You will settle for par.

If you are lucky, you will get a birdie or an eagle.

But, the ultimate is the HOLE IN ONE!

I am searching for my HOLE IN ONE!

I am a mom first and foremost. I have three beautiful children, ages 22, 18 and 13. I share custody, so they are away from home 3 days one week and four the next. This allows me time to pursue my career and date (although, I haven't done much of that lately).

I am employed at a local special purpose government as the Accounting Manager. I supervise four accountants and I love my job. I get to travel some as part of my job, and that has been a nice perk. I recently studied and passed my Certified Government Financial Manager exams. This was part of my long term career goals. Step one! Ask me about my plan!

I enjoy going to my local cheers, having a few margaritas, dancing, singing (don't get excited, I am not that good....just fun).

I love the summer time and going to the beach. I enjoy hanging out with my daughter and her friends because I feel like a teenager again (and who doesn't like that feeling). My sis lives in Lake Lanier, GA and I love going to her house because it's like being on vacation. I am closest to myself when I am there. She is my hero.

In the fall, I love SEC football and cooking hot wings for the games! On Saturdays, my TV is always on a game. Being a numbers fanatic, I enjoy keeping track of the scores and stats and who is going to the SEC and the BCS.

My parents died when I was younger, so I am not faced with the responsibilities that many of you have at our age (taking care of elderly parents). Don't get me wrong, I would trade places with you any day!

If what doesn't kill you makes you stronger, then I am one strong lady. I have been faced with my share of life's mishaps, heartaches, heartbreaks, broken promises and letdowns. But I don't stay down! I will throw the small things away. Handle the bigger things as quickly as possible, and get on to the GOOD STUFF! Life is too short. JUST DANCE!

If you are viewing my profile, you don't mind someone who is 40-something, aging, hopefully gracefully, but not without my share of life's little aches and pains. After all, our bodies are just a machine, requiring preventative maintenance and a little TLC, of which I don't get enough of - I am hoping you can provide some motivation!

I am looking for the southern gentleman and the old-fashioned courtship. Just because mediums of communication have changed, doesn't mean we can be rude and disrespectful. If you are honest, caring, romantic and supportive, let's talk. Take me out. Get to know me. Let's have fun! Say what you mean and mean what you say. At our age, there are many of us still raising children. There are many of us whose children are already grown. We are all at different stages of our lives. Neither of these are a deal breaker for me. I will get to know your children and respect you for being the devoted, dedicated father that you are. Just as I anticipate the same. Should your children be grown, then I congratulate you for this accomplishment!

Being my age, I am looking for my life partner. Someone to grow old with, retire with, have fun with. I want my best friend. We will all have baggage, and that baggage has molded us into who we are today and it will follow us. I am looking for someone who recognizes that this baggage is part of who we are, but we love each other "because" of who we are, not "in spite" of who we are.

I love my job, my home, my family, my friends and the peace that is inherent to where I am today. I am looking for someone to accentuate that peace; to share the good times and blessings that God has given us in this world.

If you see something you like and think we may be compatible, IM, favorite, email. You may find that I am an aggressor and may pursue you. When I see something I like, I go for it! But if you aren't interested...just tell me...

So Let's Get Out Here and Find our "HOLE IN ONE!"

Sandy

So there we have it! The profile of Bamagirlluvsu. And it is great, don't you think? The golf analogy! Wow, incredible! How many men in this world play golf? And how many will be impressed to know that I know the terms "birdie" or "eagle" and can use them in the appropriate context in a sentence? I actually wrote this about ten years ago for a guy that I was dating at the time. I thought I would impress him with it. (And it impressed him so much, that he is no longer here either – LOL).

And then I tell that I am a mom first and foremost. That must be made perfectly clear up front. My children are very important to me, as with any parent. So I get that one on the table immediately. And then my boring profession has to follow. It is a part of who I am. So I share that because I must show my intellectual side. I am successful in my career and others should know that. So I go on to tell about passing my Certified Government Financial Manager exams and then throw out the interrogatory! "Ask me about my plan!"

I am sure you read the entire profile already, as most men do online. (If you didn't, it is okay. You can go back and read it now. Really. Now!) Smiling! Sometimes they don't read it at all. So I won't bore you with the why's and what's and the how's of each entry to my "about me" section. I simply wanted my dates to see a little of all sides of me and to know that my sexual, sensual side is important. But that is the icing on the cake (wanna lick?). The other parts of me are so much more important. Because anyone can lick the icing, but it takes a pretty special person to bake and serve you the entire cake!

Just Dance! Yes the reference had to be present in my profile. "I Hope You Dance" by Lee Ann Womack© is my favorite song. This song will be played at my funeral. I have three books about this song on my night stand by my bed. Each of the books has a CD in the back. One each for my three children so that they all have a copy and no-one should have an excuse about where a copy of that "dang book" and CD are, when the time comes for the beautiful rendition of this song. (Unless the "CD" is no longer a medium of music...I mean, I hope to live a very long life and I am sure with ever-changing technology, the term "CD" will be obsolete).   The words describe who I am down to my inner core. I don't give up. I don't give in.   I WILL NEVER LET ANYONE OR ANYTHING LEAVE ME BITTER! I WILL JUST DANCE!

Song Application - "I Hope you Dance" – Lee Ann Womack©

Here I am online, searching for a new man. I have been married way too many times and don't even know if that is an option for my future. I want someone to love me and have fun with me and treat me like I matter.

I am also afraid that I don't have a youthful body to offer.   Once.   Once when I was like in the ninth grade, I weighed 98 pounds. But now, the body grew slightly (I wish). Metabolism slowed down. I have war injuries remaining from the three children that invaded my body. And wrinkles. Wow, the wrinkles. Caused by those same children and the previous men in my life. So, I must illustrate that to people (I am so brutally honest), without making myself appear to be self-conscious or insecure.   What resulted in my profile was my beautiful paragraph about "aging gracefully" and the body needing a little "TLC...and preventative maintenance." That is great! Priceless! I just let everyone know that my body has it's little breakdowns....and needs work....and isn't perfect....and I asked them to provide some motivation for me to get my lazy butt up off the couch and do something about it! Priceless!

I am seeking a southern gentleman.... someone to respect me and be loyal. That paragraph had to be added. Later. Much later, after my dating rituals began. "Take me out".... "Let's have some fun." Yes. All added later. Because I discovered pretty early into my online dating saga, that there are a lot of men on these sites (and women too, I am sure), that are really only seeking a one-night hookup. After a few of these guys and the presumptions and assumptions that go along with the evening, I decided to interject this paragraph into my profile. Respect was warranted.

I believe I did it and I believe I did it well. I believe I touched on all parts of my personality. I illustrated I am a Mom, I work hard, I play hard, and I love with all I have. I believe in priorities and I believe in a balanced life. I believe you can see ALL of that in my profile. If you can read, that is. And if you don't get so tired by the time you get to the end, that you never see that I signed my real name to the profile and your first question you ask in your email inquiry is "What is your name?".. . Duh! You didn't read the profile, did you?

LET'S GET OUT THERE AND FIND OUR HOLE IN ONE!

FORE!

LOOK OUT CYBER-WORLD, HERE I COME!

♥♥The Entertainer (Scott)♥♥

It was one of those nights. I had a very long week at work. Stressed. Yes, it was definitely a margarita night! I thought I would visit my friend Gail (you will learn more about her later) for a few margaritas, a little karaoke, and a little dancing to relieve a week's worth of stress. So, I dressed in my black and red dress, to match the black and red camaro, and I headed out!

Gail had the ideal place for a social gathering. An outside bar with a hot tub, television, complete kitchen, and a karaoke system, of course. Everyone always wanted to hang out at Gail's place, so you never knew who you would meet there. On this one particular night, I walked into the outside bar, and Gail said, "Sandy, come sit by me." So, I did. Not recognizing, that sitting in the seat to the right of me was a guy that I had never met before. He was not particularly attractive, I thought. At least, that is what I thought at first. Then, the more we talked, the more he made me laugh. And laughter is important. Then he sang a song. Wow, this man could really sing! He had a great voice. He began to dance and move across the dance floor in a way that grabbed your attention. "He is an entertainer," I said.

I recognize that this story is not about an online dating experience. But, I felt it necessary to throw in a few of those "fix-ups" and relationships that occurred before and during my on-line dating period. These relationships were a part of what made me who I am and set the framework for my expectations of others.

"Fix-ups?" You know the ones. When a friend or family member has someone that you just have to meet! They are perfect for you! So, on this night, I am not really sure if this was a prearranged "fix-up", or if we both just happened to be there that night. But on this night, I met Scott, the Entertainer. Yes, I shall call him Scott.

Scott was easy. He was laid back. Simple. Nice. He was very respectful and caring, and he made me laugh. At this point in my life, this was exactly what I needed. He sat next to me on the bar stool and he seemed to be so into me. The way he looked at me. The way he would say something and then laugh. His laugh. Yes. Captivating. He would reach out and touch my leg (after all, I had on that black dress…my legs were showing for a reason). He would touch my leg and look at me timidly and say, "Is that okay?" Well, yeah!

So, Scott and I had a great time that night. Then he walked me to my car. We stood at the car as he kissed me. And kissed me some more. And some more. With a few margaritas and the attraction definitely in the air, it was very difficult for me to walk away from this man's advances. But, I did. After all, this is small town, Alabama. And everyone makes it their business to know everything. I was not going to be the girl that went home with Scott that night. Scott gave me his number and I drove away.

Scott thought that was it for us. He told me later that he wasn't used to the "nice girl." Scott was accustomed to meeting the girl, steeling her heart (at least for the evening) and taking her home. When I just got in my car and left, he thought that was the last time he would ever hear from me. But, I was a little captivated. And the easiness of the attraction was pulling at me. I had been in a disastrous relationship for five years with a man that I could not carry on a conversation with, without it resulting in anger. So to be able to talk so freely with a man that could make me laugh instead of cry was a huge draw for me.

Scott was important in my development as a single, divorced woman. He was important in making me realize that someone can be good to me. He came into my life just shortly after my divorce. He was my revelation. He didn't have a lot of money. But, that wasn't important. Scott had character and that was worth so much more. He was so intrigued by me. I made him feel something that he had never felt before. No-one had ever appreciated him for who he was.

So, I did call Scott again. The very next night. "Meet me," I said. "Meet me at Logan's." Really? Yes! So, he did. He arrived at the restaurant and we kissed. We went inside and had a few drinks. Then Scott walked me back to the car. We decided to take a drive to a nearby park, take a walk, and talk. Once we arrived at the park, I will confess that there wasn't much walking or talking. We sat in his truck for what seemed like hours. As a matter of fact, I think it was hours. Laughing. Talking. Kissing. Wow! A lot of kissing. Scott could kiss like no-one. Again, he was so into me.

Did I dare let him touch me? Did I dare let it go further than the kiss? I have always said that the kiss is important. After all, if you can't get passed the kiss, there isn't much chance for anything else.

So, he began to get more sensual with me. Like when you are a teenager and you have never been intimate before. Experimenting for the first time with various touches and maneuvers in a truck, trying to bend this way and that way. Twisting and turning. Sighing and moaning. Wanting. Desiring. Saying no, but wanting more.

Yes, I wanted Scott. My body ached for him. The desire was so strong. My mind was racing. What should I do? I am single. He is single. "Just go home with him!" I told myself. But my mind was battling this. "If I go home with him now, it may be too early. Men seem to crave the chase. Once they have captured their prey, the slaying is done. And they walk." So the battle continued between my mind and my body as the heat radiated from my skin.

I stopped. "No." I said. "This isn't the time. And definitely isn't the place. Although, feeling like a teenager again is kinda fun. But, let's wait. The timing will be better. And the place will be more comfortable and relaxed. I am going home." I know Scott was disappointed. I was disappointed myself. But proud. Proud that the desires of my body did not overtake the logic and reasoning of my mind. Yes, I made a good decision that night. A really good decision. I drove away feeling proud, yet still longing for more.

The Trailer Park

After we arrived at the trailer park (did I say that out loud?), Scott had bought a bottle of wine and I recall us attempting to open the wine. I must admit, I am not an avid wine opener myself. I wasn't brought up around wine, so opening a bottle of wine would have been a chore for me as well. But to watch Scott open this wine gave a whole new meaning to "you might be a redneck if"… "If you open a bottle of wine with a screw." No, not a corkscrew…a SCREW! He had no opener at all. So we looked around the house (trailer), until he found his improvisional screw. Watching as it took every ounce of his strength to push the screw into the cork. Then wondering how he was going to pull it out. But he did. And we laughed. Priceless, I thought. Simply priceless.

The search for the wine glasses came next. Now, you have to know that if there was no wine opener, there certainly were no wine glasses. Scott had an improvise for that as well. He had purchased one of those boxed sets. The NASCAR kind. And it had a couple of glasses in it. Not exactly wine glasses, but it wasn't a red solo cup either. So we were ready.

We sat on the sofa drinking wine in the trailer hood. We laughed and had a great time as we talked about the wine opening and the waterbed. The waterbed? Do they still make those? Well, let's just say that it was a waterbed frame and it had a mattress inside of it. The bed stood three feet off of the ground, so one had to climb up and over to get inside. Also, there was the added romance of lighting. Yes, lighting built right into the headboard. Designed by Mr. Scott himself. This was great. A great evening. Relaxing. Non-pretentious. Normal. Mmmmm. Okay. Not so "normal." But it was fun. And it was easy. And I left that night smiling.

Baggage Revealed

Sitting on the sofa one evening came the news. The story of his past. The baggage. It follows us all, doesn't it? Some of us are lucky enough to put the skeletons in the closet and pray they never surface again. But, Scott had a past, a past that I might hear about one day. Scott felt it best to reveal this past to me before I heard it from someone else and then I might not get the real version of the truth. I might receive the "blown up gossipy" version of the story.

Scott began, "When I was eighteen years old, I had a girlfriend. This girlfriend was sixteen years old. Her parents found out we were having sex, and I was arrested. I spent six months in prison. Then I was released on ten-year probation. After ten years, if I satisfactorily completed my probation and received nothing else on my record, then the felony crime would be reduced to a misdemeanor. I completed my probation and the charges were reduced."

Wow, I sat and listened to Scott's story. This act and this accusation could occur with either of my boys any day of the week. This is what I constantly do. I always put myself in someone else's shoes. I can empathize that way. I can see the big picture. I can KNOW how things can happen and they could happen to me. Or in this case, this could happen to my young adult male children. I felt sorry for Scott. At least he was honest with me.

Scott proceeded to show me the paperwork that supported his story. He was so afraid that revealing this past to me would somehow change my opinion of him. That this story of "rape," even though statutory, would change the way that I felt about him. Our relationship would be over. He was so relieved that I was able to be empathetic. I could open my heart and know that he was telling me the truth. I believed him. And I believed his heart. This man had such an incredible heart.

The truth was revealed. Proven. And accepted. Nothing could hurt us now.

UNTIL:

Concerned Sis Investigates

My sister, Belinda means well. She always has. She is younger than I am, but she has always been the strength of the family. When I told her about Scott, she asked me, "Sandy, did you do a background check on him?" She knew that I had not. So she did. Then came the telephone call. "Sandy, what are you thinking? This man is on the federal sex offender website!" I went on to explain to Belinda that I had seen the paperwork. The charges were dropped. He should not be on this site.

I called Scott to tell him. He was appalled. He began to tell me that earlier that month the local county office had called him to come to the office to register. He carried his paperwork to the office and explained to them that the charges had been reduced to a misdemeanor years ago. This charge should have never followed him across state lines. The lady in the county office explained the process to Scott. Scott had to go ahead and register. This was a state requirement. But, she assured him that he would never be placed on any list, state or federal. He would be given an opportunity to appeal his case to the State before any publication would occur. Obviously, with the sudden appearance of Scott on the federal website, this opportunity was never granted to him.

Wow! What a mess! I told Scott I would help him. I am the Google© queen, you know. I immediately began to Google© the laws and the requirements for registration. Apparently, the State of Alabama has the more strict laws of all states when it comes to sex offender registration. According to the state law, if you are ever required to register, then you are always required to register. This isn't fair. Not at all. I felt sorry for Scott. This is over twenty years later. He should not still be punished for a bad judgment call made at the age of 18.

My mind reverted back to my teenage boys. Wow! This could be them. They could have a girlfriend younger than them. Their hormones (yes I said "their" – it takes two!) could rage and sexual activity could occur. The same thing could happen to them. Except. Wow! Get this! In the State of Alabama, this would not be a crime. The legal age of consent is 16. So Scott is being punished in the State of Alabama for an action that would not even be a crime here, for something that occurred over twenty years ago in another state.

So, I Googled© to determine what Scott could do to resolve this? I sent letters and emails on Scott's behalf. I really did not know this man at all, but I recognized his heart. And this man was genuine in all aspects of his life. He was a true giver. He had never allowed this negative part of his life to bring him down. He continued to maintain a positive attitude and it showed in his actions and in his laughter.

Scott went back home to appear before the courts to have this expunged from his record. According to the law in the state in which the alleged crime occurred, the crime had already been reduced to a misdemeanor and there was nothing more that they could do. Scott had to deal with the State of Alabama directly. He sent his appeal to the State. And he waited.

Aaron's 499

Scott and I had planned to attend the Aaron's 499 race a week later. Scott loved racing. He lived, breathed, and slept it. He loved Dale Earnhardt, Jr. He was his favorite. But, in my mind, I had begun the battle about what I should do. Scott had only been in my life about two months. This was definitely not a long-term relationship. Feelings had begun to emerge, however. The comfort level was definitely there. But the battle between my heart and mind was raging. I had a little girl, a daughter of eleven years. How could I continue to see a man that was on the sex offender registry? I had pre-planned the breakup. And it was going to be hard. I already knew that Scott had strong feelings for me. So this would definitely be hard.

We went to the race. I could not take that opportunity away from him. He was as excited as a kid at Christmas. And he enjoyed himself just as any child opening their gifts on Christmas morning. He was up cheering the crowd on. The entertainer inside him was definitely present.

My sister and her husband had brought a guest with them to the race. A very handsome, flirtatious man. He was very attractive and was obviously attracted to me. He flirted. I flirted. And Scott noticed. And Scott questioned. I brushed it off.

That was crude. That was wrong. How could I be on a date with Scott and flirt with someone else? Perhaps, the pre-decision to break up had something to do with it. My mind already knew that I was going to break up, so it made it easy to flirt with someone else.

The Breakup

When the breakup occurred, Scott did not understand. He felt that I was judging him. He also felt that I was only breaking up because now I was interested in the other gentleman that I had met at the race. I kept trying to explain that I had already decided to break up prior to going to the race. But I wanted to allow him to enjoy that time. I explained to Scott my reasoning. "I am not judging you. I have seen the documentation. I have seen the proof. But....I live in small-town Alabama where everyone knows everyone. All it will take is for one person to see you on that website and my daughter's dad to find out, and he will take her away from me. It has nothing to do with the truth. Allow one mother to find out that I am dating you, and my daughter's friends will no longer be allowed in our home. I cannot do this to her."

Scott tried to understand. He wanted to believe in me. He knew we had something special together. This was hard. I told him it didn't matter what the truth is, it is the presumption of the truth that would guide actions toward me.

I have managed to remain friends with Scott and I still hear from him occasionally. The last I heard, he had hired an attorney to pursue action with the State. There were many repercussions that followed his appearance on the sex offender website, including his neighbors being notified. Scott also lost

39

his job. Things got a lot worse before they got better. Scott finally acquired a job, met someone, and has relocated to another state. He no longer has a physical address in Alabama. I sincerely hope that he is happy.

This relationship meant so much to me in so many ways. I was allowed to open my heart up again for someone that needed to be loved. Scott and I cared for each other. We were there for each other at a time when each of us needed someone. I also learned that the judicial system isn't always fair. Of course, I had heard that all of my life. But, I had never truly witnessed this myself.

Scott is truly a wonderful, kind man and has suffered a lifetime for a bad judgment call at the age of 18. I still empathize with him. Many may not see my point of view. I believe that we are not to judge - innocent until proven guilty. Scott's innocence was turned to guilt by a bad judicial system, varying state laws, and the need of a daughter's parents to make him suffer. The parents, I am sure, did what they felt was right at the time. And I wonder, if the 16-year old girl of so long ago, would think differently about the actions that she and her parents took back then.

The Entertainer. He is still out there! Positive. A heart of gold! And he is still fighting a judicial system that did not give him a chance to live! Hang in there, Scott! "It's what you do!"

♥♥Anyone Need a Little Viagra?!♥♥

It was a hot, summer night in Miami Beach, Florida. I was on a "sister trip" with Belinda. My sister trips are always great! A lot of laughs. Fun! Fun! Belinda and I went into the bar at the Marriott. A nice, little sports bar. This was a training trip for my job, as well. Several people from my industry were in the bar. The band was playing. We were dancing. Having a great time!

At these meetings, there are always vendors in attendance that are there for networking purposes, to make contacts for their businesses. This meeting was no different. There was a vendor in the bar (we will call him George – and he is in the....window business....yeah ....that's it. George from Georgia was selling windows). So I just protected the guilty. Smiling.

The ambiance was great! We were at the beach! Miami! Laughing! Drinking! Dancing! And there was George. George wasn't the greatest looking man in the room. He wasn't ugly. He just wasn't the best looking. But he could dance. I recall him performing the "Michael Jackson" moonwalk as good as Mr. Jackson himself. He was fun. He had an outgoing personality! He loved to talk. Of course! He is a salesman! That is what he is supposed to do!

And, yes. There was the flirtation. He looked at me with "that look." You know the one. Like he could eat me up! Yes, and I am sure he could. We all sat at the table, drinking and talking. Belinda always demanded the attention of the room and she always received it. She could take a dead room and bring it to life in an instant! That is just who she is! So there we sat with the room now alive! Belinda had gotten the party started.

After several drinks and way too much fun (you can never have too much fun), George slipped me his room key. "Come to my room, later! We can watch a movie!" he said. Is that what they call it these days? LOL. Smiling. I slip the room key in my wallet, not yet having decided if this is an invitation that I want or not.

As the evening continued, with a little more tequila, and a lot more dancing, and a whole lot more flirting, the thoughts of going to George's room crossed my mind more and more. But, I was just not sure about what I wanted to do.

It's Miami. It's hot. The music is blasting. Belinda looked at George's arm and noticed a tattoo. What is that? She looked closer. "What is this date on your arm?" she asked, recognizing the recentness of the date. George didn't try to hide it at all. He actually revealed the truth. It was his wedding date! Yes. This man was married! What! He gave me his room key! Now, nothing would make Belinda and me madder than a man cheating on his wife. Belinda told him what she thought. In only a style that Belinda could do!

What was that? In the corner of the bar stood a strangely dressed man. He didn't seem to fit into the crowd at all. After all, on this given night, the bar was filled with business people. So, when the man appeared, dressed all in black, with large jewelry draping from his neck and arms, it was obvious that he wasn't part of the crowd at all. He stood in the corner, alone...and quiet. As people walked by, he was handing them something. Very discretely.

George came back to the table with one of the samples that the strange man was passing out. Samples? Samples of what? Viagra! Wow! What a concept! A pharmaceutical representative in a bar passing out samples of Viagra! (Perhaps, he should throw in a few condoms with that)!

This had been a really great night, in spite of finding out that George was married. I always have fun with my sister! (After all, we can have fun in a shoebox)!

Belinda always has the best ideas! The most intriguing ways of retribution. George had really ticked Belinda off. "Sandy," Belinda said, "Why don't you give George the Viagra and tell him to go to the room and take it and that you will be up shortly?" Mmmmmmmm. What an idea!

So that is what I did. No, I did better than that! I must ensure that George take the Viagra. He must! He has to! I walked up to George and in my sweet, sexy voice, whispered in his ear, "Hey baby, I have a terrific idea. Take this little blue pill for me. We will go to your room in a few minutes, and I am going to rock your world." I continued with more passion and excitement in my voice, "You see, George, I have been drinking tequila all night, and tequila makes me horny. It will make me do things to you that you have never experienced before! Here, George! Take it." To provide a little more persuasion, I nibbled on his ear and gently stroked his inner thigh, as I pushed his hand toward his mouth with the little blue pill. I whispered, "Take it, so you can take me....all night long." George took the pill, oblivious to what would happen next. My duty was done.

I know that you guys can see exactly where this is going. Belinda and I had no intentions of me going to that room that evening. Belinda knew exactly what she was doing when she suggested this and she used me to do it! This man had to be punished for his proposed infidelity. He probably picked up a different woman in every town that he travelled. He had to be stopped!

George returned to his room alone that night. Waited. I am sure patiently at first....and not so patiently later as the affects of the little blue pill appeared. George must have taken care of business himself that evening, while Belinda and I lay in our beds and laughed our butts off! Sweet is revenge!

Drinks on Me

The next evening, we returned to the bar again. There sat George. What? Did he not learn his lesson! There beside him was a tall, beautiful blonde. She had all my legs! Wow! Gorgeous! And George sat with his arm around her smiling. He was at himself again… the affects, and perhaps the memory of the little blue pill, were gone. He was working on round two! As we passed by, I looked over at George and said, "Hey George, did you have a **hard** time last night???" Belinda and I snickered to each other and kept walking. The look of fear in George's eyes said it all!

We were seated at a table and ordered drinks. It wasn't long into the evening that Belinda got really generous! "Drinks on me! Hey you, wanna drink? Drinks on me tonight!" Then Belinda was ordering drinks for everyone. "What are you doing?" I asked. "I just feel a little generous tonight," she said. "Drinks on me!" she bellowed!

Okay. Whatever. This wasn't like Belinda. I mean, Belinda is generous with her money when it comes to family or close friends. But, these were total strangers. I really did not understand at all!

When we returned to the room that evening, I asked Belinda, "What is wrong with you? What were you doing tonight?" Belinda smiled and said, "I didn't pay for drinks tonight…George did!" I looked at her with disbelief and said, "Really? You didn't? How?" "He gave you his room number," she said. "Seriously! Did you really do that?" I inquired with more disbelief. Belinda, with that mischievous look in her eyes, replied, "I am not going to say that I did, but I

44

am not going to say that I didn't. But, hypothetically, if I did, do you think he would ever say a word? Would he want his wife to know?"

Wow! Double Jeopardy! Belinda just made George pay for the same crime twice! Priceless!

Song Application - "Maybe Next Time, He Will Think Before He Cheats!" – Carrie Underwood©

♥♥My Bernie Journey♥♥

On a hot, summer afternoon, while attending training in Miami Beach, Florida, I met a wonderful man. This is the story of a new beginning. Bernie tells this story best and I love to hear him tell it. But I will try to tell this story with as much excitement and enthusiasm as he does.

(Okay. I will interject here. You are probably thinking to yourself, "When is she going to get to the on-line dating stuff? That is why we are here!" Be patient. I assure you, there is plenty to come. These first few stories are important to my growth into the single world. I would not have been prepared for the on-line dating realm had I not experienced these relationships first…). The story continues…

It was June. It was Miami. And it was HOT. I walked into the training facility expressing that emphasis. Bernie later told me that he thought to himself… "Well, yeah! It's June! It's Miami! Does she know where she is?" I knew where I was. I had just walked a good distance in the heat to my training facility. And there sat Bernie on the couch in the lobby. I sat down beside him and noticed immediately that he had a Blackberry. A Blackberry! Wow! I had lost my charger and my phone was almost dead. Bernie saved the day!

Bernie offered to take my phone with him to his training and plug it into the USB port in his laptop. And he did. How thoughtful! And Wow! Did I do that? Did I give a strange man my cell phone? What was I thinking? At the time, I had no anxiety over that (and I should have). He was gone maybe an hour and returned to the door of my training room and knocked. I gathered my things and left the room. His training room had flooded due to the storms outside. And my facilitator did not show up.

So, it was 3:00 in the afternoon and we both had excuses…I mean reasons…to leave our training. I asked him if he would like to join me in the bar for a margarita…and he did. That was the beginning. And it all started over a Blackberry! Bernie and I sat in the lounge and talked and talked and talked. We enjoyed our first margaritas together and talked about our baggage…or our "luggage" as Bernie called it. This was just the beginning of us getting to know each other.

I should add here, that Bernie was from New York. He was in Miami as one of the facilitators of the training. He was a "Yankee" and he talked the talk and he walked the walk. He was Italian. Don't get the wrong picture! He wasn't the beautiful, Italian guy that would sweep you off your feet, just from the first glance into his eyes. He didn't have the physique of a male super-model. His beauty wasn't obvious to the naked eye at all. As a matter of fact, when I sat down next to him on that sofa, I was truly only interested in his telephone charger. But, the story would continue about how the Alabama girl met the New York guy. And with nothing in common, closeness would evolve from two hearts reaching out for love.

After the margaritas, later that evening, after dinner, we returned to the bar with my sister, Belinda. Or was it "Miranda," my sister's alter-ego? "Miranda" appeared in Gulf Shores, Alabama, many years before. She is the side of Belinda that appears when necessary to take care of certain situations, or to be the very vocal part of my sister. Don't get me wrong, Belinda can be very vocal. But Miranda …well…Miranda will get pretty crude. She will say just about ANYTHING! I believe that Bernie met both Miranda and Belinda that night. We enjoyed delicious chocolate martinis. YUM! (After Belinda told the bartender how to make them). Bernie didn't drink one with us. He just watched and listened as we enjoyed the scrumptious drinks. Licking the chocolate from the glasses. Laughing. And enjoying each other.

I got my first kiss from Bernie that night…he thought it wasn't just right…so he made a second attempt. And he got it right that time…Oh yeah! He GOT IT JUST RIGHT! I did not go to the room with Bernie and he never expected me to. He was a complete gentleman. We were staying at the same hotel, just a few floors between us, but we had just met. And even though the attraction was there, the timing was not right.

The next morning, I awoke and went to Bernie's room to walk with him to the first training session. I walked in and sat on the bed as he was preparing for his next class. We talked. Kissed. And Kissed some more. I must say this right here. Bernie could kiss. He could kiss like no one had ever kissed me before. His kisses were the most sensual of any kiss that I ever had.

The sad time arrived. We parted ways. We had met. Over a Blackberry (I never did find that charger by the way – divine intervention). We had a few drinks. We went for a swim. We went to dinner that evening with Miranda/Belinda) and talked. Bernie did most of the talking. Well, he and Belinda. They talked a lot. I mostly listened, learning everything that I could about this man.

We went back to the hotel bar that evening where we enjoyed scrumptious chocolate martinis and Bernie took the time to listen. To watch. He said that he listened to Belinda and I interact. And we laughed. Giggled. As two sisters would. He didn't know what we were laughing at, but he laughed right along with us. He enjoyed watching us. He said he had never seen or heard anything like the two of us together.

My laugh: he described as "contagious" …just like my friends from high school. He loved to hear it. "You are my angel from Alabama," he would say. WOW!

Yes, this was definitely a new beginning…for Bernie…and for me. We were both at a time in our lives when we needed each other. We met because of a divine intervention from God. I believe that. God brought us together for a reason. And that reason had to be discovered…explored…

Bernie was a wonderful man and I left Miami Beach, Florida with sadness. And an excitement. Where would this lead? Where would this go? I did not question if I would hear from him again. I knew I would. I somehow just knew.

And I did. We spent the next several weeks with phone calls, texts, Facebook©. Anything we could do to stay in touch. We even discovered Skyping© together. We talked and we talked a lot! About everything. We were soaking it all in. Getting to know each other. Learning about our past. Our children. Our families.

Bernie was an astounding man. He sent cards and little gifts. Trinkets of his affection. The first gift received in the mail. Simple and sweet. A wind chime. A wind chime to remind me of "sunnier days ahead." We met at the beach after all. It must symbolize the beach. And it did. Sunshine and palm trees. He also sent my daughter something. A way to a mother's heart is through her children. A turtle and a key chain. Both reminders of the beach. And then a box of taffy for us to share. As I said. Simple and sweet, but truly gifts from the heart. This was my Bernie and this was just the start of our sweet journey.

The second gift…just as sweet…just as much thought. A chain for my car. A car chain. The chain was an off-circular shape with the letter S swinging inside. A crystal charm from the base of the chain to catch the sunlight while driving. This chain still remains in my car. As I drive to work, it catches my eye and I am reminded of this man who came into my life with such a zealous and selfless attitude. Such thoughtfulness!

We Will Always Have Chattanooga

One month after meeting Bernie, we agreed to meet in Chattanooga, Tennessee at the Chattanooga Choo Choo. This was exciting and scary. Bernie and I had met, so it wasn't completely a blind date. But this meeting was to be our first time alone together. No Miranda or Belinda around to help hold the conversation.

I was scared. Anxious. I asked myself over and over, "What are you thinking?" I didn't really know this man. I did. But, I didn't. What was I to expect?

I arrived at the Choo Choo before Bernie. I went to the bar and had a margarita and explored the place. The closer the time approached for Bernie to arrive, I got more and more nervous. I felt like a kid on the phone calling every few minutes and asking, "Are you here yet?"

Finally, Bernie arrived. He took me in his arms and placed the most sensuous kiss on my lips. He let me know how much he missed me and how glad he was to see me. Bernie, being Bernie, brought little trinkets of his affection. He brought two books about New Beginnings and Life. He also brought New York t-shirts for my daughter and me. Oh yes... and we must not forget...he brought a "relationship foundation" gift... a phone charger. This was Bernie. This was who Bernie was and would always be. He always showed his affections. He loved giving from his heart...And he always did!!!

We spent the weekend together, learning and exploring each other. We had wonderful conversations. Walks. Talks. And kisses. And, it was this weekend that our relationship would become more grounded. Bernie had been married his entire life to the same woman and had never had an opportunity to explore relationships with other women. I would be his first "other woman" in years. The kisses were hot. And many. The sensuality of those kisses was such that it didn't matter if we took this desire to the next level or not. Bernie's kisses took me places I had never been before.

Continuing with our tourism outreach, we went to downtown Chattanooga, after buying a GPS for my car...after all, if I am going to be on the road traveling to see my Bernie, I must have a GPS...AGAIN – Bernie being Bernie. (Later I would discover that the GPS would become my self-empowerment tool. It would allow me the comfort and freedom to jump in my red camaro and seek new friendships). We walked through shops. Laughed. Stopped to watch a couple of young adults dancing to the steps of the waltz on the sidewalk. Bernie praised them...just Bernie...

We had lunch at a street-side bar/grill with a bloody mary bar (never knew there was such a thing). I had a margarita. Again. More laughter. More talking. Holding hands. Exploring. Learning. Still just the beginning of our relationship. The more we talked, the more we learned. The more we laughed. The closer we became. We will ALWAYS have Chattanooga!

The next evening, we decided to go to the Station House. The interesting, unique thing about the Station House is that the servers sing while they are serving you. They will bring your wine, and then scurry to the stage to sing. And the singing wasn't that bad. Actually, it was pretty good. We ordered too much food. Filets, shrimp, more shrimp, salad, wine...as I said....way too much food!

But, it wasn't the entertainment. It wasn't the food. It wasn't the fact that we were listening to music from our era (the 80's). It was the fact that Bernie and I sat across the table from each other and smiled. Laughed. We knew the songs. We could talk. We could relate. This was a very valuable part of our "getting to know each other" time. We held hands across the table.

Bernie said all the right things. How special I was to him. How much he was growing to care about me. How I was his angel from Alabama. Bernie was beginning to like me....really like me. LIKE LIKE ME! We were making our first memories together. Real memories! Lasting memories! This was just the beginning of my journey with Bernie!

When we left the Station House, we stopped at a gift shop to look around. I realized that Bernie had left my side and was at the front counter chatting with the clerk. As I approached the counter, the clerk asked me to excuse myself. I walked out of the gift shop and went to the restroom. When I returned, Bernie was walking out of the gift shop. We stopped for a moment to sit on a bench. Bernie handed me a gift box. I opened the box to reveal a key chain. But not just any key chain. It was a heart shaped key chain, glass, so that you could see through it. Inside the key chain were multiple charms. Charms that Bernie picked out himself. Charms that Bernie proceeded to explain:

The two hearts symbolize us....together

The green emerald is your birthstone

The "S", of course, is your initial

The cross symbolizes your faith

Then....The Choo Choo......Because....WE WILL ALWAYS HAVE CHATTANOOGA!

The Journey Continues

So, Bernie and I returned home to our "other lives," knowing that we would always have Chattanooga and longing for the next time that we would see each other. We returned to the world of texts, phone calls, Facebook©, and Skyping. This was the first time that we realized that life was going to be hard…that being away from each other would be hard.

My next days were filled with longing to see him. And of course, Bernie being Bernie sent roses. Roses to say everything! Everything from "I miss you," "you're wonderful," "you are a friend," to "I am glad you are in my life." These roses said it all. They said it all because there was something different about them. He knew yellow was my favorite. But it wasn't just about buying my favorite flower. Anyone can do that. Bernie had to be Bernie, the unique person that he is. The person that gives from the heart. Bernie sent yellow roses (knowing they were my favorite). But sitting right in the middle of eleven yellow roses was one single, beautiful red rose.

Wow! Wow! Wow!

The symbolism. Our relationship was new. Yellow, not only being my favorite, symbolizes friendship. And that is where we were in the newness of our relationship. Friends….but more…The single red rose symbolizing the newness of our love. YES! That is what this was growing to become! A love like none either of us had ever experienced. YES! This was still the beginning of my wonderful journey with Bernie!

The next week, I was taking my children on vacation. Bernie and I arranged for him to come down and spend the day with us…meet my children. This was very exciting and scary for him. Would they like him? Of course they would! Bernie came to the condo. He brought breakfast. We spent the day at the pool…. laughing… talking…. he learned about the children, interacting to get to know each of them. That evening, he took us all to dinner at Pineapple Willie's and we ate ribs. Wonderful ribs, overlooking the ocean. And, again. It wasn't just the food. It wasn't the view. It was none of those things that made this special. It was us being together. Watching Bernie get to know my kids and watching my kids interact with him.

After knowing Bernie about a month, he came to North Alabama to see his Alabama angel. This again, was a time of anxiety for me and him. He was coming to my home. To my space. He would see where I lived. He would see me on a routine, daily basis with my children. He would see more of "me." The workings of who I am.

Bernie made everything okay. I was very comfortable with him. He cooked for us. He went to the grocery store and bought everything that he would need to prepare an enormous Italian feast! YUM! We ate and ate! AND of course we had leftovers for later! And, by the way, I cooked for him as well. He had the opportunity to try a southern favorite…Chocolate Gravy! No-one can make chocolate gravy like I can. I was taught by the best, my dear sweet Mother!

Bernie…being Bernie… brought everyone a small gift from his travels to New Orleans the week before. His gifts were, as usual, very well thought out. He brought things specifically unique to each of us. A margarita sleep shirt for me. A box of Mardi gras beads and a mask for my daughter, a USS Alabama flask for my 21 year old and a t-shirt meant only for my 17 year old. Bernie had taken the time in Panama City to get to know each child….and it was apparent in his gifts. And that is just who Bernie is!

Sandy: "Bernie you are amazing."

Bernie: "I am amazing because you make me feel that way."

Bernie: The four-letter word used to describe our relationship: DAMN – "Damn – Love times a billion."

Sandy: Speechless

Bernie: "Apollonia – the lightning strike" – In other words, we have it bad!

Bernie: "I am so much in love with you that my heart wants to leap out of my chest."

Bernie: "We have a helluva journey ahead of us."

Sandy: "And I am looking forward to that journey."

My journey with Bernie…My Bernie Journey….corny, cheesy, but it was an awesome journey. It began as a journey filled with love, hope, and a fulfillment of dreams. Each of us was there to help the other one through a time in our lives when we needed someone. Bernie was just going through a divorce after a lifetime marriage. He hated losing his family. I came along just in time to help Bernie believe in himself again. I was at a point in my career that had grown complacent. Bernie helped me believe in myself again. He encouraged me! He provided me with an inspiration to pursue my Certified Government Financial Manager certification. (And I later did). Bernie also gave me the inspiration to write a book (not this one….the inspiration for this book came later). He helped me to earn my self-pride and self respect again, to believe that I am worthy. Worthy of so much more than my past. He gave me the inspiration to dream again. To have a plan for my future. Thanks, Bernie. You are truly a wonderful, giving, spirited man. I could not write this book without the chapter on my journey with Bernie. He set the standard by which any other man in my life would be judged. No-one could treat me less than the way Bernie treated me. I deserved nothing less.

The inevitable. The ending of this relationship came. It wasn't easy. But as I began to realize that I wasn't in love with Bernie, I had to let him go. I knew that keeping this relationship going under false pretenses would only hurt him more. Bernie, deep down, knew it as well. We have been able to maintain our friendship, knowing that we gave each other what we could and what we needed at the time. And now we have a lifetime friendship remaining. The first person that I called when I passed those CGFM exams was my sweet Bernie. I knew that, without the Bernie Journey, I would have never had the courage to believe in myself and pursue a long-term career goal. I would never believe in dreams again! Everyone truly comes into our lives for a reason. I will always be Bernie's Alabama Angel!

**Song Application – "Kiss an Angel Good Morning"
– Charlie Pride©**

♥♥(F)emale (S)oul (M)ates – My FSM's♥♥

What would a woman be without female companionship? Her friends? Those that laugh with her, cry with her, relate to her in every way. They finish her sentences. Things that they say to each other that result in hysterical, gut-wrenching laughter make no sense to the male population around them. If these partners in crime were male, this book would not be necessary. The fishing expeditions would never have occurred. I would have found my life partner, many times over. My female soul mates, (my FSM's) are my partners for life.

My girlfriends made it very clear that there had to be a chapter dedicated to them, the women in my life. My sisters, my daughter, my friends. My FSM's. These beautiful girls play such an important role in my life as my encouragers, my worriers, my matchmakers, my laughter creators, my tear driers, my friends. These ladies are truly an inspiration and have inspired me to be better. Not just a better person, but a better friend. If I am just half the person that either of these girls is on the inside, then I am one awesome lady. Smiling again.

My FSM's have helped me, through their words, their phone calls, their texts, their jokes, and their uplifting reiterations that I am important and I matter in this world. They helped me to discover that my heart is filled with faith and hope. I am encouraged that there exists that one male counterpart for me. The man that will lift my spirit like no other and help me to see the person that I am. He will love me with all he has and be glad to do so. He will see my heart. He will get me and what I represent. And when I am laughing with my girls, he will sit across the room and smile, knowing that we aren't talking about him. It is just what we do. And this man of my dreams....knows that. And he loves me and understands that it takes a lady's FSM's to complete her.

Song Application – "Run the World (Girls)" – Beyonce©

Just Keep Swimming (FSM 1)

Ten years ago I had the opportunity to meet Gail. We had a mutual male friend. This friend, Kenny, says, "Sandy, you have to meet Gail. The two of you are so much alike that I know your personalities will connect instantly." And they did. Gail and I knew instantly that we were meant to be more than friends...more than sisters. We were female soul mates in every sense of the word. We could look at each other across the room and instantly know when the other one was hurting on the inside. That is what a soul mate does. Knowing the other person's needs with them having to say nothing takes a phenomenal closeness to each others' hearts and thoughts. Gail and I have this closeness and it is a grand thing.

I won't ever forget one of the first nights that she and I went out to our local bar as they hosted "Working Women's Wednesday." WWW. Yes, it was a place for women to gather after work, on hump day, to try to relieve a little stress and get through the remainder of the week. Local businesses contributed door prizes. There were drink specials. And all of your friends could gather for a few drinks, a lot of laughs, and a little dancing (man I stayed skinny back then...dancing is great exercise). And, of course, where there are women, there WILL BE men!

An old friend from high school, we shall call him Thomas, was there. I had so fallen for this man. I don't quite know what the draw was to him, but it was there. I decided to not include our story in this book because that story would make an entire book in itself. Thomas became my comfort zone. The man I would always return to, and it was always the same story, re-written a little differently each time, but always ending the same way. Thomas would always end up with someone other than me. I finally gave up on him. But, on this given night, Gail had never met Thomas. Then she saw him. She said to me, "Sandy, that guy. The one with the toupee!" "Toupee!" I said…. "I didn't know he had a toupee! I pulled his hair….and it didn't come off!" Gail and I have laughed so much about this over the years! I never see the forest for the trees!

During the beginning of our friendship, the movie "Finding Nemo©" was released. You know the one…the children's movie where the small clownfish gets lost in the big wide ocean. This movie became the foundation for our friendship. It is the epitome of what Gail and I represent. Having experienced a life of heartache and disappointment herself, Gail knew what it was to be lost in this big world, wondering why things happen the way they do. But Gail, like me, always picked herself up off the ground and "kept on swimming." She is a very courageous woman that continues to battle life's disappointments, but it never matters what is going on in her own life, she will be the very one that shows up to help you get through your current heartache or letdown.

I recall one Sunday afternoon; I was going through one of my "feel sorry for myself" days. I picked up my phone and I sent a text message to many of the friends in my life. I didn't want to get out of bed. I don't have many days like that. My strength won't allow it. My children need me. I am a survivor, so I throw the small stuff away, handle the big stuff as best I can, and get on with my life. There is always tomorrow. But this was one of those days when I felt like I had taken all I could take. I was depressed. I sent the message, lay back down in bed and covered my head.

The next thing you know, Gail had appeared at my bedroom door, a plate of food in hand, and a shoulder to cry on. We sat there and she cried with me. She allowed me to cry as many tears as I needed to cry. Then we picked up the computer and I began to show her some of my on-line prospects, and some of my on-line "you gotta be kidding me" not so much of a prospect kind of guys....smiling. We laughed and laughed and laughed some more, as I searched to find "squirter guy." When I was finally able to dig him out of the "blocked" area, Gail looked at him and said, "Awwwww, he ain't all that"....and we laughed.....Deep down that FSM side of us came into play as we both knew... yeah....He was all that. But looks did not matter at this point. Because some things are just more important. He was definitely a happy NEVER after.

When I broke the news about my book to Gail, she was so excited. The shrill in her voice as she said, "Oh, Sandy, this is great! And you are so good at this! You can do this! Yes, you can. And...don't forget, when you make it to Oprah's Book Club, I must be your Gail!" Priceless. But, it could happen. Gail went on as she continued into our dream world, and played out an entire scenario of me and my FSM's all appearing on the Oprah Book Club. As we began to share our stories, Oprah says, "Okay girls, the Springer Stage is next door." Gail is grinning as she continues to play out our Oprah outcast story and says, "I can see Jamie standing up, taking a puff from her cigarette and marching toward the door saying I told you that we went through the wrong door!" Funny. Gail can always make me laugh. Making it to the Oprah Book Club would be a dream come true. In the meantime, I can just laugh with Gail as she dreams the dream with me, her FSM. She is truly my "Gail."

Gail and I can be sitting outside at her poolside bar and be talking and laughing. Gail has the ability to take anything negative and turn it around and make a positive from it. I guess that is why we complement each other so well. Gail's voice, her accent, the way she lengthens her words, as any gorgeous southern belle would do, adds to every word that projects from her mouth. She can be saying what she needs to say, and her head will begin to sway backwards and forwards. Now you know that it's on. Oh yes. Someone or something has really pissed Gail off. And she feels the need to let you know about it! Especially if it is with regards to the "underdog" in any situation. Gail is always going to pull for the underdog. The one that no-one else understands or tries to understand. Gail will help the poor, the sick, the lonely, those in need regardless of the need. She will defend with all she has. She will let her opinions be known, and do so in such a way as to make you laugh about it. You will be laughing….and then crying….and then laughing again. And Gail will look at you and say in her sweet southern brogue, "Just keep swimming…just keep swimming."

And we always do…. Thank you Gail, for always being here for me. You are a true friend and FSM….

Granny Amy (FSM 2)

I have known Amy for about ten years now. When she and I met, we discovered we had been dating the same guy. It was quite a funny story and since it involves Thomas (the guy that I am not putting in this book because his story would take an entire book) that bonded us even more. Amy and I have experienced many failed relationships together. Each of us always here to catch the other one when we fall.

Amy is the true friend. She knows ALL about me and she loves me unconditionally. She is a realist and sees the best in everyone, just as I do. We may go weeks at a time without talking or seeing one another, but when we do, it is always easy for us to pick up right where we left off. I don't know what I would do without her.

Amy is my constant. She is the one friend that never goes away. Through thick and thin. Through it all and back again. She is written into many of the stories throughout this book, because she is that constant friend. You found her referenced in my profile when I uploaded pictures. She was the friend that invited me on that free trip to Las Vegas (the one that cost me $2,000). We experienced Phantom of the Opera together. You will find her referenced again in the Canadaman chapter as we play dress-up at a charity cancer event.

Amy is the lady that any good man would want to find. She is responsible (has a good job), she knows how to have fun (i.e. – Las Vegas). She is loyal (hence why she is my constant). She is a great mom (with two beautiful daughters) and a terrific grandmother (thus the Granny Amy chapter title).

My heart would be a little less complete today had I not met Amy ten years ago. Thank you, Amy. You are the ultimate, forever FSM.

The Original FSM (FSM 3)

The original FSM is not the "oldest" or hasn't been around the "longest." As a matter of fact, she is my newest friend. She earned the "Original FSM" title because she became the girlfriend that was there when the "Female Soul Mate" acronym was born. It was her personality connection with me that drove my brain to reach as deep as it could reach and push the words "Female Soul Mate" up to my lips.

I met Kathy at the ball park. Our daughters were playing softball together. Kathy had a very outgoing personality. She was a lot like me. We aren't quiet. Just the opposite of that. Very, Very opposite of that. She and I don't care what others may think of us. There are so many people who become introverted because of worry about what others may think. They will shut down. Maybe it is the small-town mentality that has driven them to that point.

But not Kathy. And not me. Together, we were the storm that attacked the ball park. We yelled. We cheered. We laughed. We even joked about some of the other mothers and how they looked at us. How they really didn't know how to enjoy themselves and have a good time. I wouldn't say we were obnoxious and I also won't say that the other parents at the ball field won't say we were obnoxious. I can't speak for them. And we do live in small-town USA.

Kathy could look at me and instantly know what I was thinking. This is tough. Especially for a new friendship. Kathy made going to the ballgames fun. Well, more fun. She enjoyed talking with me and hearing my stories. When she found out that I was participating in the on-line dating rituals, she began to be the "fix-up" person. She had two men that were the "perfect guy" for me. Yeah, right!

Now, don't get me wrong, Kathy knew some really good-looking men. She would show me their pictures and I would be in awe of their beautiful appearance. There was only one problem with the men that Kathy attempted to fix me up with. They were TAKEN! They always had a significant other in their life. Kathy had taken the time to really get to know these male friends and she knew what was best for them. They were unhappy in their current relationships, but like some people tend to do, they had gotten comfortable. And even though they were unhappy, they couldn't leave the existing relationship. Each had their reasons.

I commend Kathy for trying and for believing that I was all of that. She promoted and sang my accolades to these guys and they reiterated back to me that "Kathy was right. You are incredible." But, I just wasn't THE ONE!

Kathy, I enjoy you so much. Thanks for being my new, caring friend and FSM. I am looking forward to many more ballgames with much laughter and conversation. As you continue to read my mind and we smile at each other and everyone else around us looks at us like we are crazy, I will continue to laugh and be loud with you. Because, quite frankly, life is too short to do otherwise.

LOL

My Co-Pilot (FSM 4)

Is it possible in this lifetime, to meet yourself? Honestly, can you meet someone that you believe is your re-incarnation, only you aren't dead yet? Or have you been? Mmmmmm? Another book in itself.

Jamie is different from me, yet the same. I met her at my Cheers and we didn't become friends at first. I watched her from a distance. She was confident. Beautiful. She came to the bar with her husband, Stan. Jamie and Stan were there each night to relax, have a few drinks, and relieve the stresses of the week. They were taking care of Stan's ailing father and children at home, along with jobs. So stress-relief was needed by the end of the week.

Jamie would play pool with some of the men in the bar and she could really kick butt! She also would play poker against some of these same men and kick butt there too. She could sing like there was no other. She had a beautiful voice. So I watched Jamie and I listened to Jamie. From a distance. She had an air of independence about her. She had an air of grace and style. I am searching for words to describe the internal, subconscious assessment that I had concluded in my brain about Jamie. For some reason, my brain had come to the conclusion that Jamie was "above" me. Better than me. Not in my league. I did not know Jamie.

Later, and I don't quiet recall when it happened, I proved to my brain that it was wrong. Jamie was not at all like I had envisioned or concluded. She was so different. She was down to earth. Outgoing. Unselfish. A loving, caring and devoted wife (and Stan was a loving, caring, devoted husband as well). Over the course of time, as I ventured into my "Cheers" and had several mini-conversations with Jamie, there came the one night, that Jamie and Stan's traditional table became my traditional table. "Our table." Our spot in the bar.

Jamie and I began to sing together. Well. One song. I guess that must be my next song application for the book.

Song Application – "Does He Love You?" – Reba McEntire and Linda Davis©

The first time that Jamie asked me to sing this song with her, I felt complimented. You see the difference in Jamie and I when we do Karaoke....Jamie is GOOD! I sing just because I like to do it and make jokes that Karaoke isn't about being good. Karaoke is about having fun. I never wanted to follow Jamie, because that made it worse. You never want to follow someone good when you are singing Karaoke, unless you are better. There was little competition in the "Cheers" bar, so for her to ask me to sing with her was a compliment in itself.

Jamie and I got closer and closer the more we got to know each other. She understood me. And for me. Watching Jamie with Stan was a blessing in itself. They were so good together. They took care of each other the way that a husband and wife should. I missed not having that. I was envious.

Jamie made it her personal quest to find my Mr. Right. She planned many "fix-ups" for me. Many of which aren't in this book. The Baby Daddy was one of her "fix-ups" and if it weren't for the fact that the Baby Daddy was the "baby daddy," he and I probably would have made it. That was a wise choice.

The fun part of watching Jamie was when she would become my co-pilot. My wing-man. Or I guess I should say, My Wing Girl. LOL. She would walk up to my next potential date, lean over and whisper my praises in his ear. I never knew everything that she said, but part of her "wing girl" speech went something like this. "Hey. Let me tell you about Sandy. She is a wonderful lady. She drives an awesome camaro, has a great job, and lives in a really nice house. And…I am not a lesbian…but if I was…I would so DO her." The guy would always laugh. It was the way that Jamie spoke the words, with such an emphatic tone. She meant every word she said. If the guy didn't want me after that, then there was something terribly wrong.

Jamie made me laugh. A LOT! I got closer and closer to her and Stan. I spent many days at her house at the pool during the summer and many nights at the bar with them. Laughing. Drinking. Singing. Jamie became the FSM that took care of me. She knew me. She worried so much about me when I was taking my road trips to meet my potential dates. That is why she jumped in with her "fix-ups." She wanted to get me off the road.

Thank you, Jamie. For the many nights that you worried about me. For the many attempts that you made to fix me up with someone to get me off the road…and to try to find someone to love me as much as Stan loves you. Your efforts did not go unnoticed. Thanks, most of all, for loving me and for being my "wing girl." It is not your fault that the men in this world didn't listen to your speech. I thought it was incredible…and from the heart. You preached my praises as only a real FSM could do.

Vicarious Living (FSM 5)

Going to work every day and keeping your life outside of work a big secret was difficult to say the least. So what did I need to do? What did I have to do? I had no choice but to find that one special person at work…the one girl that I could trust to be my Co-worker FSM. That person became Jessica. Jessica was the perfect person to become my FSM at work. She had been married for many years and loved to listen to my stories.

Jessica was the type of person that didn't want to be on the road. She would not have put herself in my shoes any day. She was married and had a man at home. But, she loved to dream about the fact that if he wasn't there, where would she be? Jessica would come into my office on Friday and say, "Hey Sandy. What are WE doing this weekend?" She loved living her life vicariously through mine.

I recall the time that Jessica and I went to the beach. When we arrived, there was a huge dragon fly in the room. It was so big that we called it the "dino-fly." Jessica was the brave one. She took the broom and began to swipe the large dino-fly from the room. I stood behind the door and watched. And screamed. We laughed so hard that I literally pee'ed my pants. When you begin to age, and you have had three children, and your bladder has fallen, well…let's just say it doesn't take much for you to laugh so hard that you pee your pants.

On my last birthday, Jessica bought me a birthday card that said, "To the friend that laughs so hard with you that she pees her pants…and then laughs with you because she pee'd her pants." Wow…a true FSM. I love Jessica and the fact that she is always there for me. She is truly the one person at work that I can trust to tell everything. I never have to worry that she will reveal or talk about anything that I say. She is proud to be my FSM. I could not make it through the long days at work if I did not have her loyalty and commitment to me as my FSM. I love you, Jessica! Thank you so much for your dedication and loyalty and for living your life vicariously through me!

My Izzy B (FSM 6)

Izzy is my beautiful daughter. She is a thirteen-year old, beautiful girl. Not a child; not quite an adult. During my five year marriage, I lost a lot of time with my daughter that I can never get back. This was a time that Izzy and I should have bonded. But, this was stolen from us by a man that I brought into our lives. I thought that I could love this man enough and he would see the love in our family. This love would change his heart. He would not be so hard. He would not be so bitter. He would not be so angry. I was wrong.

I can't go back in time and relive these years with my daughter. Though, I wish I could. We all have those moments of regret that we can't do anything about. All we can do is forgive ourselves for our bad decisions, accept the forgiveness, and move on. That is what I have done the last two years. I have moved on.

Spending time with my daughter and her friends is like being a teenager again. And who wouldn't love that feeling? My teenage years were taken from me as a result of an ailing mother. I was forced to have to work or my family didn't eat. My income was necessary to provide food and shelter for my family. So, I worked 48 hours each week and went to school. Where was my childhood? Why was I deprived of this time in my life? Another part of life that no-one can explain. So, we lift our heads up and move toward the future.

So, I have an opportunity to relive a childhood that I never had. Izzy and her friends have allowed me this time. They "let" me participate in their activities. Sometimes, I believe Izzy wishes that I wasn't around so much, but her friends think I am cool. They love getting in the red camaro and going on road trips, with the window down and stereo blasting. And Izzy loves it too. I can't begin to tell you how many pictures we have made of the girls hanging their heads out of the sunroof as we cruise the streets of the neighborhood.

The first summer after my divorce, I devoted strictly to Izzy. We had so much fun that summer. We visited Belinda at Lake Lanier. We went to Panama City Beach for vacation and she took a friend with her. We visited Point Mallard Water Park at least three times that year. Taking pictures of the snake that appeared once. It was nothing for us to jump in the camaro and take off.

I asked Izzy to describe why she liked cruising. She didn't say much. She knows that getting in the car and driving anywhere...even if it is just to McFarland Park on Sunday afternoon, that we have a free spirit. It is great to roll those windows down, open that sunroof, turn the radio on....and drive! Our hearts are open to the music and we sing and smile and laugh with each other.

In January 2012, I received an opportunity to go to Orlando, Florida for class to prepare for my Certified Government Financial Manager exams. I asked Izzy to join me. We were going to be gone for eleven days. I told Izzy that she could bring a friend along. Izzy said to me, "Mom, eleven days is a long time. Two girls will fight. This is too much drama. And...also, they would want to stay up all night, sleep all day, and we would sleep the entire vacation away. No thanks, Mom. I would rather go with you." Wow, what a mature response.

Izzy and I spent those eleven days in Orlando and it was great. We had an opportunity to bond like we had never had before and will probably never have again. I asked Izzy, "What is the one really big thing that you would like to do while in Orlando?" Izzy replied, "Is the Magic playing?" And yes they were. The Magic was playing the Lakers that weekend, and Izzy and I must go. We ordered tickets online and we saw that game. Izzy was priceless. She had to have a Lakers shirt. And she sat among thousands of Magic fans and cheered for the Lakers. She was so much fun to watch as she bellowed out, "Go Lakers" each and every time the crowd chanted, "Go Magic." I love my daughter. And our time was a grand one.

I told Izzy that we would do one more big thing while in Orlando. Money was scarce, so we had to pick and choose. There is so much to do there. Izzy said, "Mom, can we go see Luke Bryan? He is in concert that weekend as well." My response to Izzy: "Baby girl, Luke Bryan is in concert all the time. Everywhere. He will probably return to Huntsville again, and we will try to see him then. Let's go to one of the parks instead." Izzy did not like the idea of going to a park. She was too old for that! She wanted to go see Luke Bryan. I finally had to resolve the issue the good old-fashioned, democratic way. You chose one night. I choose the next. So we went to Universal Studios. And Izzy soon discovered that no-one is ever too old for the Orlando parks.

Nights in Orlando were especially fun. Cruising International Boulevard in the camaro. Yes. I definitely have a song application for this one. This song seemed to be on the radio every time we got in the car.

Song Application - "International Love" – Pit Bull©

Our time in Orlando is one that I will never forget. I told Izzy that we should stop and thank God for allowing us this time together. It is an experience that we will always have and no-one can ever take that away from us.

Izzy is a sweet, gentle soul. Her innocence is still within her heart and her body. And she still wants Mom around. There will come a time, and in the not too distant future, when Mom won't be important anymore. Izzy will be more involved with friends. And boyfriends (oooohhhh.... scared of that one). For now, I will soak up every moment that I have with her, knowing that tomorrow it can be over. It doesn't matter how many times Izzy looks at me with the embarrassing eyes, or tells me to shut up. There is always that glimmer of love behind those looks. The glimmer of love that tells me, everything is okay between us. She is my daughter and I am her mother. This is the best combination of an FSM that anyone could ever have.

I look forward to watching my Izzy as she matures into a beautiful adult woman. I know that time will change her. Heartbreaks will temporarily crush her hope and faith for love, just as they did mine. These things are inevitable. But what no-one can take away from my Izzy is her ability to look at me with that glimmer in her eyes and say, "Shut up, Mommy," and I will know that it's just my Izzy. And that she loves me! She is the ultimate FSM.

Song Application – "In My Daughter's Eyes" – Martina McBride©

I Can Have Fun in a Shoebox! (FSM 7)

What can I say about Belinda? She is my sister and my best friend. Belinda has always been there for me. Always. While I have had a pretty tough life, losing my Mom at the age of 18 and my dad five years later, compound that loss by deducting six years to obtain Belinda's age. She was 12 and 18. She literally grew up with no mother. But, she had me. We had each other. And we both had our older sister, Sue. Sue was the one that had to take care of all of us while Mom was sick. She was the strong-hold of the family.

Belinda and I have a sister relationship that is beyond comparison. She is always there to listen to my horror stories and she never passes judgment. She has been my life. My hero. My friend. She has also been the best aunt that my children could ever ask for. My children always went to spend a week with her each summer. The joke now is that the kids have to go to Belinda's boot camp when they get out of line. Belinda can always bring them back to the era of respect and honor that they should have anyway. She is the strength that holds us all together.

Belinda has always said to everyone, "If any of us sisters are to get cancer (being fearful that one of us might), then it will have to be me. I am the strong one. I am the mean one. I am the one that could beat it!" And Belinda is right. We hope that none of us ever have to go through that, but in the event that any of us do, Belinda knows she could stand up and fight...and she would WIN!

Belinda loves with all she has. She has a kind and giving heart. She sends money and gifts to third world countries to help the poor and the sick. She helps serve food at Thanksgiving to the hungry. She will help friends in need with monetary or health problems. Belinda is the one that truthfully, unselfishly gives of herself.

Having witnessed death of both parents before she was 18 years of age, this became Belinda's weakness. She has a very difficult time going to funerals or watching someone die. Even with watching her pets suffer or die, Belinda becomes weak and melts underneath a waterfall of tears. She simply can't deal with the reminders of the pain and suffering she witnessed at such a young age.

Each morning, during my commute to work, Belinda is the person that I call. I have to check in and let her know what is going on in my life. Work, kids, and whatever man is in my life. Belinda always listens and offers the best advice. She loves me. And she is concerned for me. There is nothing that Belinda would want more than for me to find the man of my dreams and be happy.

Belinda will read about many of my adventures for the first time as she reads "Bamagirlluvsu." Routinely I share EVERYTHING with her. But the road trips and adventures taken by "Bamagirlluvsu" would only have worried Belinda. So I chose to keep a lot of these adventures to myself. Belinda will be okay reading these stories after the fact. But had she known about them at the time, I would never have heard the end of it. Not because she would feel the need to control the situation, but because she would have worried about me. I did not want her to worry.

Belinda has an alter-ego. Miranda. Miranda was born in Gulf Shores, Alabama, on one of our trips. Miranda is the person that comes out, when necessary, to clear the air...to get things right...to set things straight. Miranda is needed...and necessary.

I love my sister. My hero. My friend. She is the FSM above all other FSM's. She was born into it and she has to accept it. But she chooses to accept it, not because of birth, but because of love. It is what you do as family.

The saying, "I can have fun in a shoebox," comes from Belinda. Belinda can truly have fun in any situation and at any time. There doesn't have to be a lot of people. There doesn't have to be a lot of money. All that has to be present is Belinda. She can walk in a room and the attention migrates toward her. It is who she is. She has the charismatic personality that attracts everyone.

Belinda has the ability to be empathetic in any situation. If you laugh, she will laugh. If you cry, she will cry. If you get down, she will...tell you to get OVER IT! Seriously, she will empathize with you for a brief moment, but having had the experiences in life at such an early age and recognizing that there is always someone worse off than you, Belinda will tell you real quickly to take a strong hard look around. You will always find someone worse off than you are.

Keep your head up! Go out in the world! And if life throws something bad your way, get rid of it...jump in that shoebox...and have fun! Because everyone can "have fun in a shoebox" once they achieve the correct mentality to do so! Thank you, Belinda, for being my sister, my friend, and my FSM! I love you! Without you, I would be lost!

The Big Sis (FSM 8)

Sue was the older sister in the family. She is nine years older than me and fifteen years older than Belinda. Sue is caring and loving and she was the one responsible for raising us while Mom worked. She did all the laundry, cooked, cleaned and "watched the children."

Sue resented having to do this at such a young age, that she almost didn't want children herself. Sue and I have grown apart over the years, although there is no reason to explain why this has happened. She can't explain it and neither can I. We have discussed this with each other. And on occasion will talk about doing something to fix it. Good intentions seem to never get us anywhere.

Sue and her husband married in 1972 and have been married since that time. She is my envy. I will never have what she has and I wish that I could. Sue is blessed to have a life partner to grow old with and take care of each other. Nothing can take that away from her.

Sue will know very little about these stories as she reads the book. I don't want her to take offense. There is no reason she should not know. She is my older sister and I am grateful for all that she did for us growing up. (Sue was the one responsible for ensuring that our family had a good Christmas each year). The important stories. The ones that meant something…Sue will know about. She will read and she will know that I shared with her the ones that touched my heart. The others were life-learning lessons, but the ones that touched my heart are the ones that I felt the need to share with Sue.

Sue, thank you. Thank you for always keeping your heart open to me and for loving me. Thank you for being a special FSM, even though I don't always show it or always tell you. I love you, big Sis!

The Hair-dresser (FSM#9)

My hair-dresser is more than just my hair-dresser, she is my friend. She is not the friend that I "party" with, she is the friend that I count on. She will always listen to me and smile with me. She laughs with me as I tell the stories about my life. I can't wait for my monthly visit to the "hair-dresser." (Yes, I have to go once each month…I can't get gray hair…I can't look old)!

My hair-dresser has been in my life for many years. We have two sons the same age. We have experienced watching young boys go through puberty the first time. We have experienced a lot with our boys as they mature into the young men that they are today. We have laughed with each other as we share our stories about our sons.

A few years ago, Miss Mona was diagnosed with breast cancer. She handled this with grace and style. She became the person of strength that I always knew that she was. She stood strong in her faith as she battled this horrible disease. And, of course, it was this same strength that allowed her to survive.

I recall when she lost all of her hair (a hair-dresser losing her hair, that would be like an accountant – me – losing my numbers….smiling). Miss Mona was beautiful. She wore a wig for a while, and then she would take her wig off and show off the balding head beneath. She would make a joke. Laugh. And move on. This did not get her down at all.

Mona is one woman in my life that I always described by saying, "They don't make them like her anymore." She is the epitome of what a real woman should be. She is everything! A great mom. A great wife. A great daughter. A great sister. And a great friend.

I love you, Mona! My FSM. My friend. I can't wait for another one of those incredible head massages. I attribute those massages as the reason for my brain being able to release these words to the paper upon which they are written… LOL!

The Rest of the Best

There are so many women in my life but I cannot continue adding pages. Please don't feel left out if you are one of my FSM's and don't find yourself portrayed in a section. Just because you aren't written on paper doesn't mean you aren't written in my heart. (This goes out to: my bartender, my co-workers, my daughter's friends, and anyone else I may have failed to mention...I love all of you)!!!

Introducing……(drum roll please)…..

THE FISH!!!!

©™*(POF)*

(IT'S ABOUT TIME!!!!!)

♥♥The Bridge to Nowhere♥♥

Online dating was tough at first. Before I changed my profile to include a little bit about all sides of me, I didn't know what I was doing, or even who I was trying to reach. I only wanted to find the right person for me. I made several contacts. I would find someone that I thought looked interesting. I would send a short email. Something like: "I love your eyes" or "You look good in that shirt" or "I love your profile." Something short and simple. Then I would favorite the person. I would also comment on a picture that appealed to me. I was very aggressive in my efforts and was even told that I was.

Once I made the initial contact, I would chat. Chatting was difficult too. Sometimes the connection would not be very good, and the slowness of the responses was aggravating and frustrating. But eventually, you could get to a point in the communication process where you knew whether or not the conversation was going to lead somewhere.

Sample Chat:

Hi, I am Sandy.

Hi, I am John.

I see you live in Birmingham.

Yes, and you are in North Alabama.

Yes, but I don't mind the drive. If I am willing to commute 70 miles for my job then why not to find the love of my life. Where in Birmingham do you live?

Oh, I didn't tell you. I am out of town working on a bridge in South Africa.

The previous conversation occurred multiple times. How many? I can't even begin to tell you. I finally asked the last person, "Really, just how many of you guys are working on that bridge in South Africa?" After that, it didn't take me long to find these guys. I could pick them out. There were varying people. But they all lived in Birmingham or in the suburbs of Birmingham. And they were all working on that damn bridge in South Africa.

Song Application – "Bridge Over Troubled Water" – Simon & Garfunkel©

Was this the same person creating multiple screen names? Or was it multiple people working on the same bridge? This seemed quiet impossible that I was selecting random people who all seemed to be in the construction industry and living in Birmingham. They all seemed to be foreign. I don't know that for sure, but their chatting would have incomplete sentences and inaccurate grammar and uses of words. I figured this pattern out relatively quickly and haven't talked to anyone working on that bridge in many months. Maybe I scared him/them away. Because I called their bluff. I would agree to meet them and they would always have an excuse.

One of the stories was quite funny. I was talking to this guy. He told me he lived in Birmingham. He had custody of his son. His online picture was with his beautiful son that appeared to be about seven years old. His son was with him this one night during our chat. He was playing a video game. As I approached the subject of meeting, I heard the proverbial excuse about working on the bridge in South Africa. I said, "Really? And you carried your son with you?" "Yes," he said. "I didn't have a choice. My son's mother left us, and I have no-one to take care of him."

Okay. So, I am skeptical about this. He carried the seven year old son to South Africa to work on this bridge. Who is keeping him during the day? So I continue with my chatting. "And who takes care of him during the day while you are working?" "I have a Nanny," he replied. We continue with our talks until the next sentence out of his mouth is this. "My daughter is ready to go to bed now." Wait a minute! Daughter! Did he just say daughter?! So, I question him. "I thought you had a son." There was a complete silence (if that is what you can have as there is a pause in the chatting session). Then his reply: "Oh, I am sorry. That was a joke. His grandfather used to say he looked like a girl. So I was playing on that joke!" Enough said. There was the discrepancy. There went the feeling of trust. Done. Finished. Goodbye!

These were my beginning contacts. I never met any of them. I could detect inconsistencies in their stories. I did not have the warm fuzzy feeling. These relationships led nowhere. Like that damn bridge in South Africa that led to nowhere. Delete. Block. You are out of here!

♥♥The Hockey Scout♥♥

Vinemont, Alabama. That wasn't far away. Just this side of Birmingham. And Wow! This man was hotttt! This was the best looking guy that I had seen online! He could have come straight out of a magazine. His name was Jeffrey. And he was beautiful! Jeffrey and I chatted online briefly. He told me about his daughter. She was five years old. There was a picture of her in his profile. He also sent me other pictures of the two of them together.

Jeffrey's story. His girlfriend, the daughter's mom, had abandoned them many years ago. Jeffrey was left to raise the little girl alone. He had hired a nanny back home to take care of her. Home was in South America. He was saddened by not being there with her. He missed his daughter terribly. He could not wait to finish his business here in America so that he could return home to his beautiful daughter. This was a very touching story…and sweet.

Jeffrey was an international hockey scout. He was here in America on business. Now, okay, so that is a credible story, I guess. Someone has to do that job! Why not Jeffrey? And Jeffrey was beautiful!

I was intrigued by Jeffrey. After all, he was the most beautiful man I had ever seen and he WANTED ME! ME?! Who could believe that? I have learned over the course of time that if something appears too good to be true, then generally, it is too good to be true. But, I was caught up in the moment. This was one of my first introductions online. I hadn't had a lot of distrust thus far. I was new. And I was searching for Mr. Right. And Wow! Did I mention that Jeffrey was beautiful?

We exchanged phone numbers. When I heard Jeffrey's voice for the first time, I was swept away. He had an accent. I can't tell you what origin it was. Italian? Maybe. I just don't know. All I know is that it was of foreign decent. The accent would pierce into your very core and pull you down under. When I tell this story, I change my southern accent to sound just like Jeffrey. And I can still hear his voice as I imitate him. He spoke like a true gentleman. A man in a romantic movie, in which the man would look deep into the woman's eyes and say, "Distance does not matter in matters of the heart." (See, as I read it out loud, my voice changed to his – incredible – chill bumps)! Yes. That was Jeffrey's words to me! And looking at his picture. He was foreign. Dark complexion. Dark hair. Dark eyes. Wow! I was captivated!

Several days went by. The telephone calls were numerous. The texts were constant. The more we talked, the more I began to recognize...something wasn't right. Damn! The signs began to reveal themselves. (Remember the accent as you read the conversation below. You must. Really! Change your voice as you read...it must sound like Jeffrey)!

Jeffrey: I am in Vinemont, Alabama.

Sandy: Scouting for hockey players? We don't do hockey in Alabama. We do football.

Jeffrey: I have some people flying in from Los Angeles to meet me tonight.

Sandy: So you are meeting them in Birmingham?

Jeffrey: What Birmingham?

Sandy: Uhhhh. The nearest airport.....

Jeffrey: No. We are meeting at the local café to have margaritas.

Sandy: We don't do margaritas at local cafés here in Alabama.

Now, this was fun. And could get more exciting. He was from somewhere in South America but he travelled frequently. He was willing to travel to see me. The next question from Jeffrey. A little scary:

Jeffrey: What would you say if I showed up at your door?

Sandy: I would probably shoot you. Not a good idea!

This series of conversations began to make me a little edgy. I told Jeffrey it was time to lose my number and to not call or text me again. But Jeffrey did not want to give up.

Jeffrey: I don't want to lose you, Sandy.

Sandy: You can't lose what you never had.

Wow, was this really happening? Was this guy really hooked? Already? He hadn't even met me yet! He continued to call. He continued to text.

Jeffrey: Oh Sandy. Please. I cannot lose you. I promise you, if you meet me, we can be so good together!

Sandy: Jeffrey, please. Leave me alone. I am not going to meet you. This conversation is over!

The conversation with Jeffrey had to be over. It had only lasted a few days and Jeffrey was acting like he had been in a life-long relationship with me. He wanted me bad. And asking to show up at my door freaked me out!

Then, I received my cell phone bill. I had over 300 dollars worth of international calls and texts. My dear Jeffrey was not in Vinemont, Alabama. My dear Jeffrey was in

Nicauraga! I sent Jeffrey a few final texts, advising him of my latest expense and demanded that he not call or texts me again. He sent a few more after that wanting to pay my bill. I simply told him to leave me alone. Perhaps he should join the others that are working on that damn bridge in South Africa!

♥♥Canada Man♥♥

When I first began my on-line dating saga, one of the first gentlemen to send me an email was "Canada man." His profile picture was that of a distinguished business man. He sat on a desk in his office, with a very large bookshelf behind him. His eyes were a beautiful, blue color, highlighted by the beautiful, blue shirt that accentuated his body. His hair was a light brown in color and was slightly long.

Canada man, we shall call him James, was obviously from Canada. He appeared in my emails when I was still a virgin fisher-lady. He is the very contributor to my changing my initial profile from a two-liner to include another paragraph. This paragraph emphasized disbelief. Disbelief that a man from Canada would want me! Me?! Why? Why would someone so far away be interested in someone from Alabama? We are all searching…looking…for something. But why me?

I sent James an email inquiring about this very LONNNNGGGG distance connection. A connection that would be more than a long-distance relationship, and I was definitely not interested in an on-line relationship. I mean, I don't mind texting, chatting, emailing, Facebooking©, or Skyping© as part of an initial on-line meeting, but eventually, you HAVE to meet. And the distance must be close enough that you can see each other at least once per week. Otherwise, there is no way that trust or commitment could evolve!

James' reply was short, sweet and simple. Unrealistic and unbelievable. His reply was that he was willing to relocate for the right lady. If he made a connection with someone, he didn't care where she lived, he would pack all of his belongings and he would move to be with her. Wow! Seriously! This was so unrealistic to me! How could I trust this?

James and I had many calls and texts to each other. He was real. The conversations were genuine and honest. He never tried to hide that he was talking with other women. He kept that in the open. After all, that is why we are all on-line. To meet the person of our dreams. We are all adult enough – mature enough – that we know that everyone we meet won't be THE ONE! So we talk to multiple, possible dates until we meet one that we believe will provide a potential relationship. James was doing the same. He was no different from me.

Then came the application. Yes…a dating application. James had met so many potential prospects on-line, and because he was willing to relocate to anywhere, he had to find a way to narrow the lot. One day, while doing my nightly "window shopping," I received an email from James. He asked me to complete a questionnaire for him. From the responses to this questionnaire, James was going to narrow his choices down to two or three possible life partners. Sounded a little crazy at first, but the more I analyzed his questions, I realized that James had a pretty good idea. He asked questions that weren't asked or addressed in the on-line profile. Simple questions, like "What is your favorite color?" or "What kind of foods do you like?" to more complex questions like "How important is your faith?" to…

This question. The one that really captured who a person was. "If you had three wishes, what would they be?" Well, I thought. I know exactly what James is trying to discover with this question. The answers to this question would reveal so much about a person. Is the person materialistic and if so, just how materialistic?

I completed the "relationship application" for James. For fun, I thought. Just for fun. I don't recall all of the questions, but that one important question that I knew would mean something to James, I answered from the heart. "If you had three wishes, what would they be?"

1. I wish I had one more day with my Mom.
2. I wish there was a cure for cancer (and world peace – just kidding – LOL).
3. I wish my children could learn from my mistakes (although, I know this is impossible; they have to learn from their own mistakes).

I was happy with my responses. I re-read them for tweaking…to make sure that I answered them the best that I could. And I hit send. Then I waited. I waited to see if I would get an interview next. Too funny. An interview to be considered for a relationship. This is priceless, I thought. I had never completed an application like this before. After I hit the send button, I really thought no more about this application. This truly wasn't like a job application, in which if you are unemployed, you are on your knees at night, praying that you will be selected for an interview.

The response soon arrived. I had been chosen. How funny. I was one of two of which James had narrowed his selection. He had already visited and interviewed the other finalist who lived in New York. I was the second finalist. We must schedule an interview. James indicated that he would fly here to meet me. I was a little afraid of that. We chatted a while longer and I told James that I just wasn't interested. It seemed a little strange and a little scary that someone would fly here from Canada just to meet me!

James had no idea of the incidents that followed. My three wishes. Could they come true? Here I am, the person that looks for signs… thus…the story continues:

Song Application – "My Wish" – Rascal Flatts©

My Three Wishes

It was a Thursday morning. I had been working a lot of overtime at work. And my red camaro, my traveling machine, was so dirty that I could not take another road trip until it was presentable. So, I went into work a few hours late that morning and ventured toward the carwash to get my car detailed. While I was waiting in the lounge for my car, a lady came in and approached the front desk. "I really need to get my car cleaned up today," she said. "I have four children and you know how kids can be. My husband and I are taking a trip to Birmingham on Sunday. You see, I was recently diagnosed with cervical cancer and I have to be in Birmingham early Monday morning for my first chemo treatment."

I was listening to the lady as she revealed her situation to the clerk behind the desk. My heart melted. She had four children and she had cervical cancer. "Bless her heart," I thought to myself. "I could not imagine if that were me." The lady came over to the bench close to mine and took a seat. I began to carry on a conversation with her. "Did I overhear you say that you have cervical cancer?" I asked. "Yes," she answered. "I did not mean to be listening," I added, "I just couldn't help myself." My mom also had cervical cancer many years ago. So I couldn't help but be concerned.

The lady sat there and began to tell her story. She was such a strong lady. Not once did she complain. She began to tell me how she discovered she had cancer. Having four young children, she could not imagine leaving this earth without them. Her husband had told her that she had to "beat this thing" because there was no way he could raise their four children alone. As I listened to her story, I was overcome with emotion. I wanted to help. With no forethought, I walked over to the bench at which she was sitting, put my arm around her and began to offer my help. "I know that financially, things have to be tough. I am not even going to ask you about this, I already know. This is what I wish to do. Allow me to pay for your hotel room on Sunday night." With an emphatic response, the lady replied, "No, No, I can't allow you to do that. You don't know me!"

I continued to plea with the lady. I really wanted to help. "Please," I said, "Let me do this. I have been blessed to travel some with my job and I have some Marriott rewards points, probably enough that this won't cost me anything. Please. Let me help." As I was saying these words, I really had no idea how many points I had, nor if they would cover the cost of the room, but it was a way that maybe I could convince her. And I did. "Okay. Okay." She said. "As long as it isn't going to cost you anything." The lady provided me with her name and telephone number and I left the carwash.

After I reached my car, I recalled that I had that long commute to Huntsville ahead of me and that I should probably go to the restroom before I made that drive. I went back into the building to find the lady sitting on the bench, crying. I stopped. Again, overcame with emotion. I put my arm around the lady's shoulder and inquired in a soft voice, "Are you okay?" She looked up at me with such tenderness and appreciation and replied, "You don't know what a blessing you were to me today." Wow! What a blessing I was to her!? She really didn't understand. So I proceeded to explain to her, "No Ma'am. No Ma'am! YOU were the blessing to me! You gave me a chance to see what my mother was going through thirty years ago as she walked in the same shoes that you are walking in today. Thank you!"

I went to the restroom. And I left the carwash that day with an overwhelming sense of humbleness. I called the Marriott and discovered that I lacked 1,000 points covering the cost of this lady's room. For $12.50, I saved this lady and her family $160.00. Wow! I was definitely where I was supposed to be that day! And all because my traveling machine needed revitalized. And all because Canada Man felt the need to issue "relationship applications." I was given the chance to relive, to some degree, what my mom must have felt to be dying, and knowing that she was leaving four children behind. Wow! (The lady called me a few months later to let me know that she was doing well. Her cancer was in remission. I hope and pray that she continues to heal, so that she can be around to spend a little more time with her family).

The next week, I received a telephone call from my girlfriend, Amy (Granny Amy). Amy's company had purchased a table at a charity auction and ball for "Camp Smile-a-mile," a children's cancer fundraiser. She asked if I would like to join her. "Absolutely!" I replied. "A chance to play dressup....yes!"

Amy and I attended this auction and ball, not knowing that we would bid on a few items, only to find that we didn't have the funds that others had in the room. We had an incredible time as we looked around the room for all the single doctors at the auction. Funny. No-where did anyone's name-tag or reserved table have the words "single doctor" on display. There was no way to tell if someone was available or not. We gave up and decided this was girl night! We danced and danced and had so much fun!

The Vice President of Amy's company had observed the fun that we were having and approached us. "Do you ladies have a room for the evening?" He asked. Amy replied to him, "No, not yet. We thought we would just play it by ear. We brought bags with the forethought that if we had too much fun, we would get a room." We were both smiling! Yes, we were having too much fun! A few minutes later, the V.P. returned and said, "Ladies, you have a room reserved for the evening, next door at the Hilton. You ladies enjoy yourself! Have a great time!" Yes, it was pay it forward time! Last week, I helped someone who needed it and it was returned to me this week! A true inspiration!

A few days later, while lying in my bed, laptop in hand, I sent James an email. I wanted to share my story with him. And I did. I love the way things seem to happen…by fate…by chance…or with three wishes. So, I began to tell James about the events that subsequently followed the submission of my "relationship application." I explained about the car wash and meeting the lady with cervical cancer and four young children. I told him about the correlation that this lady's circumstances had with my own Mother. I told him that I felt like "Wish Number One" had been met. I truly was given an opportunity to feel like I had spent "one more day with my Mom."

I also told him about the charity auction and ball for children's cancer. And about the "pay it forward" event that followed. I could not begin to explain to him how I felt! It was an overwhelming sense of disbelief and joy, all rolled into one. I know that a cure for cancer (Wish Number Two) had not truly been fulfilled; however, I did have an opportunity to participate in a fundraiser for cancer, play dress-up, and have a great time with a really special friend. It was a great week.

I proceeded to humble myself more as I continued. "Now if my children could just learn from my mistakes." I laughed. I can only hope that my children have learned a few life-learning lessons from me. My skeletons are not hidden in my closet. I released them long ago. It is best to share with your children the life mistakes that you make, in hopes that they can learn something from you. If they learn one thing…one thing at all, then it is worth not being prideful.

Canada Man, James, and I never met. Could he be my Mr. Right? I guess I will never know. I am adventurous, but not enough to trust that a man would actually relocate from Canada to Alabama. James did provide me with one thing. He gave me an opportunity to look deep within my soul and ask myself what are my priorities? What means the most to me in life? I recognized that James was trying to determine who would be materialistic and who would speak from the heart. Knowing the answer that James was expecting to receive, I still answered the way I would have answered without knowing his motive. I spoke from my heart. My three wishes were revealed…and somehow, each in their own way…my three wishes came true!

♥♥I'm Going to Jackson♥♥

Jackson. Wow! This is the first guy from on-line that I ventured out and physically met. He lived in Jackson, Tennessee. So, I will refer to him as Jackson. His profile picture was one of a beautiful, blonde man. His picture was of him on a boat. A ship. A cruise ship. It has always been my dream to go on a cruise. One of my bucket list items. And I will go. One day. Yes. This guy's profile attracted me.

The main draw to him was a one liner in his profile. Jackson preferred for a woman to make the first move. So, I did. I made him a favorite. I emailed. And immediately, he sent me his name on Facebook©. So, we became Facebook© friends. This became one of the things that allowed me to trust a man online. If someone will send you a friend request, then generally, they are real. Their Facebook© page is real. It contains their friends, their family, and their place of employment. If someone will Facebook© you, then generally they have nothing to hide.

So, I sat at home in my bed and chatted with Jackson, learning more and more about him every day. He had the most beautiful, blue eyes. So, I began to call him "blue eyes." It fit. It worked. And I was really drawn into his eyes. Eyes are the first part of a man that capture my attention (then it's the legs – smiling). The more we talked and learned about each other, I revealed where my oldest son was attending college. Jackson replied, "So is my niece." The more I looked into it, I discovered his niece was my son's friend on Facebook©. It is truly a small world.

I was beginning to find my comfort zone with this man. When I looked at his Facebook©, I found that he worked for a non-profit agency in Jackson. There were links to his company's website within his Facebook©. Pictures of Jackson appeared of him at work with his clients/customers. Yes, Jackson was a real man. I was building a trust in him.

Our telephone calls turned into a discussion about planning a meeting…a date. Our schedules seemed to always get in the way. Jackson's job required him to work a lot of nights and weekends, attending various functions. He also served as an umpire for the local little league. And, of course, my schedule was just as hectic. Finding a time that we could both meet was difficult, to say the least.

One evening around 9:00, I was at home in my woman cave, when I received a telephone call from Jackson. His children were taken care of for the evening and he wanted to see me. Of course, I wanted to see him. I immediately began getting dressed and packing a bag. Jackson invited me to come to his home for dinner. I wasn't sure that this was the appropriate or right thing to do. After all, I would be driving over 100 miles to meet a stranger in his home. This was just the opposite of what the POF© dating safety rules would advise you to do. As a matter of fact, the rules state (and this is common sense) that you should always meet in a public place. However, I felt comfortable with Jackson. After all, he Facebooked© me. I saw his employment site with his pictures. His niece was friends with my son. I felt a connection. I felt safe.

Jackson's employment also provided me with a comfort area. He was involved in a service industry that provided counseling for battered and abused children. I listened to him tell about his job and some of the things that he had witnessed and I was taken back in time to my own life. Jackson made me feel safe. Protected. The softness in his voice as he empathized with these families touched my heart. I believed that it was this very important fact about Jackson that gave me the courage to pursue my adventures in on-line dating.

The importance of this first date with Jackson is relative to all other dates because this date set the foundation for my safety. I established my own set of rules. I created a system in which I would feel safe and thereby provide me with the security needed to get in my car and travel to Jackson, Tennessee (and any other place I wanted to travel in the future).

Even though my comfort level with Jackson had already been established, I know that sometimes people can misjudge others. Sometimes our heart allows us to be too trusting, so I emailed myself all of the relative information about Jackson. I included his name, his place of employment, his address (after all, he had to give that to me if I was going to drive to his house), the number of children he had, what kind of car he drove, his POF© screen name, and any other relative information that I might have discovered during the course of our chats and conversations. Not only did I email this information to my personal email, but I also emailed this information to my work email, as well as texting it to my telephone. I did all of this and then…I told Jackson that I did it. YES! I revealed my plan to my date. After all, if he KNEW that he would get caught, there is no way that he would kidnap, rape, or murder me! He would definitely get caught! I was safe!

I went to Jackson, Tennessee that night. Anxious. Nervous. Many emotions overcame me. I honestly did not know what I would be facing when I arrived. This was my first real meeting with an on-line date. I was concerned, to say the least. I wasn't concerned about whether he would like me. I already knew that he would. I was concerned about whether I would like him. I wondered about his home and whether I would feel comfortable there. I was curious if I would be attracted to him or not. And…I questioned. I questioned why I was driving almost two hours to see a man that I didn't know. I questioned why he didn't offer to drive to see me. Why did he not offer to at least meet me half way? Was I allowing him to disrespect me? Did I appear over-zealous? Did I appear desperate?

I was out here in the single life again. I had lived through so many years in a disrespectful marriage, and I was searching for someone that would honor and respect me. Then, why was I setting myself up for another man to disrespect me? Why would I allow myself to look so desperate that I would drive so far to meet a man? This was crazy!

Yes! My mind was in a constant turmoil. Questioning and wondering. Yet I still drove. I told myself to turn around several times. Yet I still continued down that highway to meet Jackson. The closer that I got to his house, the more afraid and nervous I became. I called him. He did not answer. Now, here goes my mind again. Because, you see, I was demanding respect. I was demanding honor. And any honorable and respectful man, knowing that his woman was on a highway, late at night, driving, might run into some trouble. His woman might need help. He should honor and care about her enough to make himself available to receive her telephone calls. At that moment. The moment of "no answer" on the other end of that line, I almost turned around and headed back to North Alabama.

But, something kept me driving. Was it the fact that I had already driven so far? It was closer to drive to his home than to turn around and return to mine. I was also intrigued. Excited. Nervous, but excited. Jackson and I had already had so many conversations and I was so drawn to him. He loved his children. Being a good father was an important attribute. He also seemed to be into me. And I still had that belief that this just might be my soul mate. So, I continued down that highway to see Jackson.

Song Application - "I'm Going to Jackson" – Johnny Cash©

When I arrived at Jackson's home, I pulled into the driveway. He met me at the car. Statement number one: "You really do drive a red camaro," followed by statement number two: "Wow! You look better in person!" And so did Jackson. He was a beautiful man. Thinner than his on-line pictures. And this is unusual…right the opposite of what routinely occurs. He obviously took very good care of himself. He worked out daily. And his home was spotless! I could never imagine going to see a bachelor, with three children, and discover an immaculately clean home. But that was Jackson! "Do you have a housekeeper?" I asked him. "No," he said, "I do this myself." I was impressed.

I liked Jackson. There was an attraction there. For both of us. However, the lesson learned here was this. It did not matter that the attraction was there. There was the distance. Jackson made it very clear that he would not travel that far to see a woman. He had done this before…the long distance relationship…and it did not work.

I will have to say that I did not listen to Jackson that evening. I made several trips to see Jackson before I realized that he really meant what he said. However, you know how we women (and men) are sometimes. We put so much faith (and vanity) in ourselves, that we believe that we are special. We are different. We are that perfect person and if we just show the significant other in our life that we are willing to put them first, we are willing to drive two hours to see them, then they will fall for us, and they will totally change their viewpoint on long distance relationships. Yes, I could change Jackson's mind.

NOT! NO WAY! HELL NO!

99

Jackson never made a road trip to North Alabama. Bamagirlluvsu was not "all that" to him. And I soon discovered that. It didn't matter what I wanted to believe or what I perceived Jackson to think of me, the reality was this. I was just another girl.

One evening, when planning another road trip to Jackson, we were attempting to coordinate schedules. Jackson wasn't available on the one and only free night that I had that week. I began to question in order to determine if he could rearrange his schedule. During the process, I got this distinct suspicion that he had another date. So, I simply asked, "So, Jackson, do you have another date?"

Now, let me say this. I should not have asked if I didn't want the answer. If I wasn't prepared for the truth, then I should never have inquired about the obvious. Jackson was beautiful. Successful. And he was on an on-line dating sight where I was sure he was the subject of many, many connections. Yes, the answer was obvious. Jackson had a date!

This was it for me! Don't get me wrong, I knew that Jackson and I had no commitment whatsoever to each other. That had never been discussed to any length at all. Except internally, within myself. I already knew that I would not see more than one person at a time. It is difficult enough to keep one man happy, let alone multiple men. And having time for any more than that, with my schedule with children and work, was out of the question. I also felt very strongly about devoting time and attention to the one and only significant other in my life so that he would know the dedication and commitment that I put into my relationships. I had expressed all of this to Jackson, but he never reiterated the same to me.

I had convinced myself, as we sometimes do, that things were okay. That Jackson and I would be together. That we cared about each other. That he was as into me as I was into him! WRONG! This on-line dating experience, rather dull...nothing exciting to really convey to you...but to teach a lesson. A lesson that we should all learn, hopefully sooner in life rather than later. If someone isn't into you, they AREN'T into you and there is nothing that you can do to MAKE IT HAPPEN! We have to all be realistic in this world of dating, cyber or otherwise. Rejection hurts. It is eminent at times. We should just be mature enough to handle it, accept it, and move on! Lesson learned!

The second thought to convey in this chapter is safety! Find a system that works for you! Tell someone where you are going! Email yourself! Call and leave yourself a message! Do what it takes to ensure that you are safe. There are some crazy people in this world. Be prepared! Jackson was a special man to me. He set the framework for my future mindset in this on-line dating world. He allowed me to see that I can get in my car and travel anywhere to see anyone. I don't have to sit at home at wait for someone to come to me. However, there must be a mutual attraction.

I am not afraid. I am not scared. I am prepared to travel the highways of Alabama and nearby states to meet the potential love of my life! Life is too short and you never know what adventure you might miss out on. Thanks, Jackson, for opening my eyes to the world! Rejection hurts! But, without taking a chance, you will never know what might lie at the end of the highway!

♥♥Birmingham Photographer♥♥

"A beautiful man," I thought. His pictures captured my attention. He was an older man, but he didn't look his age. I was at home one Friday night when I discovered the Photographer. He was from Birmingham, which was only a few hours away. That wasn't so far. I am adjusted to the commute. I gave him my phone number almost immediately. He seemed so honest and sincere. And I had been online a while now. So I was much better at judging character than in the beginning.

When he called, I was amazed at the connection! It was unbelievable. We began our conversation and talked for a few hours. And everything was going well, until I saw something on his profile. Something that concerned me. Religious affiliation: His response was that he didn't have an issue with agnostics! People who didn't believe in God. Could I talk with this man knowing that he wouldn't care about my faith? This caught me totally off guard.

I sent him a message. "I need help understanding your answer regarding faith. Please explain." He wanted to do it by phone...not by text. It was important that I understand. He called me and began to explain that he didn't judge people for what they believed. Each person is entitled to their own beliefs. For that reason, he checked every box. He was not going to place prejudice against anyone for their faith.

We talked for hours on the telephone about this. He began to explain how he got to the place in life that he didn't put a lot of devotion to organized religion. I listened. And I understood. It was ironic. He had the same religious background as I had. My mother was Church of Christ and my father was Baptist. His mother was Baptist and his father was Church of Christ. As we began to relive our childhood with each other, I felt a unique and overwhelming connection to this man. He began to talk about when he was younger and he attended vacation bible school at the Church of Christ. The joy he got from going was for the free snacks and the grape Kool-Aid. I smiled inside as I recalled attending Vacation Bible School and getting to drink that grape Kool-Aid when I was a child. Being poor, this was a real treat for me and my siblings.

Having this conversation with Mr. Photographer reminded me of my own religious affiliation. I have stated that I believe in God and my faith is what gets me through the day. I know that God is protecting me and guides me daily. I was born into a Church of Christ family, and never really attended church regularly, until Mom became sick and was diagnosed with cancer. When she became ill, she turned to God as a lot of people do. It is the only thing that can allow us to pass from this Earth in peace. My father was Baptist. When he died, he had never been baptized, which leaves the Church of Christ members questioning if he has a chance at heaven. This is one of the areas that lead me to question religion.

Then there is another area. The area in which we can choose our religion to accommodate our way of life...to accommodate our sins. Each religion has its own beliefs. I changed from Church of Christ to Baptist so that I could marry again. In doing so, I was told I had to be baptized again. I had a difficult time accepting this, but I did it. Because I wanted to be married to my second husband and I wanted to begin a new life with him. In doing so, I needed to change my religious affiliation.

Over the course of time, I began to question why there were varying religions that allowed different viewpoints. It has to either be right or wrong, doesn't it? So I convinced myself that religion is simply a way for mankind to express his faith. Our God is an awesome and forgiving God and we will be judged by what is in our hearts, not by what sign is on the door of the church we attend. That is where my mentality had taken me, and that is why I could relate with Mr. Photographer. I now understood his statement.

Mr. Photographer and I laughed. Our conversation lasted until 12:00 midnight. And then 2:00 am and then 4:00 am rolled around, until finally the sun came up and 6:00 am rolled across the clock. Wow, it had been years since I had carried on a telephone conversation that long. All night long! And I didn't mind it at all. As I hung up the telephone and fell asleep in my bed, I had dreams of finally meeting someone that understood me. I could not wait to meet this man!

I had my daughter that weekend, and I never go out when I have her, so I knew it would be some time before I would actually meet Mr. Photographer. We continued to text and chat throughout the next day. Then, Izzy asked if she could spend the night with friends. I immediately contacted Mr. Photographer to see if he wanted to meet for dinner. Being the gentleman that he was, he said, "I can drive there. I don't mind. A lady should not have to drive to meet her man."

Wow, what a change. This was a totally different mindset from what I had seen before. So, we agreed to meet. He decided to drive into town and get a hotel room so that he wouldn't have to drive back to Birmingham so late. He also asked if I would pick him up at the hotel since I knew the area. I made it perfectly clear that I would pick him up, but I was not coming inside. He agreed.

I drove to the hotel, and called and told him that I was in the parking lot. I waited patiently, watching the doorway. Anticipation. Then…he appeared. I recalled thinking, "OMG, he is so fat!" And he looked old! He had on a button up shirt that was untucked and wrinkled, jeans and tennis shoes. I thought he could have dressed a little nicer. First impressions matter!

He walked to the car and got inside. I smiled, trying to hide what I was really thinking. He unrolled a picture. It was probably a 24" X 20" print. As he unrolled the picture, he made this statement, "I started to bring flowers, and then I thought that flowers would die. So, I brought you a picture of a flower, a picture that I made. This will last forever." This was such an appropriate gift from a photographer.

"That is such a sweet sentiment," I said. "I can honestly say that no-one has ever brought me a picture of a flower before." We drove to Applebee's and ordered a drink and an appetizer. We sat and talked. Making conversation with Mr. Photographer was easy. He was very easy to talk to, but I couldn't help but look around the room wondering if anyone I knew was in the restaurant. I didn't want anyone to see me with this man. He looked like my father. He was wrinkled…and he was fat! I looked like I was at dinner with my father! And I had to sit here with this man for several hours.

The evening couldn't end soon enough. We got in the car and drove back toward the hotel. As we got closer to the hotel, he asked me, "Do you want to come in for a little while?" My response was, "No, I need to get home." Then he asked, "Well, do I get to see you again?" I replied, "You are putting me on a spot, aren't you? You are going to make me tell you the truth! I had planned to take the coward's way out and send you a text message." He said, "I want to hear it from you, not in a text." So, as tactfully as I could respond, I said, "I am so sorry. I just don't feel a connection. I really wanted to. I really did. I just don't. I am so sorry."

He understood. We were both adults and we both knew that we risk this chance when meeting someone new. I dropped him off and thanked him for dinner and the picture, and I drove away. He sent me a text later stating that he returned to Birmingham that evening. He didn't stay at the hotel. His feelings were hurt. He sent several texts after that, asking what was wrong with him. He wanted to know what he did wrong. Why couldn't he find someone?

Wow, Did I totally understand how this man felt!!!! I know what it is to feel down on yourself and wonder why? After my last ex-husband left, I felt so beat down. I crawled into a hole that I thought I would never get out of. Yes, I understood hurt and pain. And I wanted to help this man to see that things get better. There is always tomorrow!

I did my best to console this gentleman. I did not want him to hurt. I couldn't help that I wasn't attracted to him. And I meant what I said when I told him that I really wanted to be. It is a terrible disappointment when you can be so attracted to someone over the telephone and then when you meet them, something is missing. I sent several texts, with my responses being that there wasn't anything wrong with him. We just didn't connect. He would find someone. I kept saying that he shouldn't give up. He eventually stopped texting and emailing. I am hoping he continued his search until he found someone that would love him. I hope that he didn't give up.

I really learned a lot from Mr. Photographer. This was my first experience with meeting someone that felt a connection with me, but I didn't have a mutual feeling. This was the first time I hurt someone else. This wasn't easy for me. But it helped me to understand better when others weren't attracted to me. It helped me to not take this so personally. This was also the first time that I had an interaction with a "false advertiser," the person that doesn't post current or real pictures online. This isn't fair to either person. I also learned to NEVER invite someone to my hometown for a first-time meet and greet. You still have to spend time in public with them and wonder if you will run into anyone you know!

FALSE ADVERTISERS DO GET CAUGHT!

♥♥Cross Country Lover♥♥

I met Rob online one evening. It was his picture that first captured my attention. He was a handsome gentleman with glasses. Then, his profile caught my eye with his words… "I am just a good old-fashioned, down to earth patriotic guy with old-fashioned values. Searching for my soul mate!"

I read further into his profile noticing that he was retired. He was 47 years old, but he was retired! That was incredible to me. That is truly a dream that we all have. After Rob and I chatted for a while, I asked to exchange telephone numbers so that we could talk. I loved his voice. It was so soothing. I must find out about his retirement. "How in the world were you able to retire so young?" I asked.

Rob began to reveal his story. He had retired due to sickness. Rob had ulcerative colitis which was an anti-immune disorder and he could no longer perform the duties of his job in aircraft maintenance. If he was hurt, it could be deadly for him. Therefore, he had relocated to Arab, Alabama, where his Mom and sister lived.

We talked so many nights on the telephone, getting to know each other. As he exposed his story about his disease and the treatments that he had to take, I felt so sorry for him. He was so young. I had known someone who had a family member that had this disease, so I had heard a little about it before now. I understood it could really be terrible and carry with it some life-changing necessities.

I began to tell Rob my story, though not as severe as his. There was a time in my life, when I had gotten so sick, that I literally thought I was dying. I awoke one morning with severe stomach pains. Diarrhea. Throwing up. Every day for about a week. Then, as suddenly as the symptoms appeared, they went away. I thought I had a virus. About one week later, the same symptoms re-appeared. I was later diagnosed as having a diseased gall bladder and had to have it removed. Then, I should be well.

However, I did not get better after the gall bladder was removed. Instead, it was quite the opposite. I continued to throw up and have diarrhea daily. I had lost so much weight and had gotten so weak, that I literally believed I was going to die. My boys had begun playing football that year, and I could not make it through any of their ball games. Nine months after my surgery, I was still as sick as I was before I had the surgery. I finally was able to get an appointment with a specialist and got the help that I needed, but it was a long time before I was at my full potential again. It was a long time before I could live life to its fullest.

I was trying to be empathetic with this man believing that we had something in common. I believed that I could relate to him as best as anyone could. I wondered about how difficult it would be for him to meet women and felt sympathy for him knowing that he was still so young. Trying to meet someone that understood his illness would be a difficult, if not impossible, task for him.

We laughed together as we discussed how pre-dating talk had truly changed. We were discussing our ailments with each other. Pre-dating discussions are now about questions like, "What medications are you taking? Do you have high blood pressure? Tell me about your health!" This was priceless. No-one could truly understand unless they had already been where we had been. Yes, this man had to be for me!

One night while talking, I asked Rob when we might be able to meet. After all, Arab was only an hour from Huntsville. This should be easy to arrange. Rob began to stutter as his answer rambled from his mouth. "I haven't exactly moved to

Arab, Alabama yet. I currently live in California, but I will be moving there this week. I have rented a U-Haul truck and am driving there tomorrow. I should be home by the weekend."

I could not understand why Rob didn't just tell me the truth in the beginning. He believed that if he had revealed to me he was still living in California that I might be skeptical about meeting him. Now, I was a little skeptical because he had lied to me. I put myself in Rob's shoes and understood. This is what I do. I trust. I believe. My heart is open.

Rob and I carried on many conversations during the next week as he drove from California to Alabama. He could not wait to meet me and the feeling was mutual. We talked a lot about each others' likes and dislikes. We revealed our family background to each other. Talked about children. Everything! After all, he had to drive so far from California to Alabama. We had a lot of time to talk.

After the long drive, Rob drove his truck home and drove back to Huntsville to meet me for dinner and drinks at a local sports bar. I was attracted to this man's personality and his spirit, but there was no chemistry between us. As we left the bar that evening, a horse and buggy drove up and we took a horse and buggy ride to the end of the street where the new Veteran's memorial had recently been built. I was glad to share the intrigue of this memorial with such a patriotic man.

Song Application – "God Bless the USA" – Lee Greenwood©

Rob and I parted ways that night, knowing the connection had not been made. He was disheartened. He had driven such a long way to make this connection. Later, he emailed me that he was moving back to California. He was not happy in Alabama. He was depressed. And he could not understand why he and I couldn't have made an effort.

I felt sorry for Rob. I know what it feels like to be sick and single and believe that you have nothing to offer to anyone. The thoughts of beginning a new relationship with someone that doesn't know you or love you or understand your physical condition. You truly believe that you will be alone for the rest of your life and that you will never be worthy of anything or anyone good. As I left Rob's life, knowing that I was one of the few people our age that would probably ever truly relate to him, I was saddened by the fact that I came into Rob's life at all. What purpose did I serve? I only presented this man with an option...an option that wasn't there. I threw him into a deeper state of depression about where he was in his life.

This was one of those times that I went home to my woman cave and crawled into my bed and began to question what I was doing. What are any of us doing? There is so much loneliness and heartache in this world. Bamagirlluvsu felt so badly that I shut my profile down for a while. I needed time to think…

♥♥The Double Date♥♥

Life is short. We pick ourselves up; we dust ourselves off, and we move on. We are each granted a certain allotment of time here on Earth and it is up to each of us to make the best of our individual situations. Laptop in hand…here I go again…

Engineer4. His screen name contained the word "Engineer" and he was from Huntsville, Alabama. Huntsville is known for its high technology jobs, so there were many men online with a screen name that contained the word "Engineer." Engineer4 and I talked for many hours and for many nights online. It was a comfort zone immediately. The conversation flowed very quickly. He was divorced, with two children, both of which were away from home for the first time attending college. He was alone and therefore, he decided to pursue someone online. Just like many of us, this would provide him an opportunity to meet new people. He worked many hours and therefore didn't seem to find the time to get out and meet people.

When Engineer4 and I first talked, he explained to me that he had just set up his on-line profile, so he was new at this. He was a "Virgin" Pof'er©. I was more than happy to provide him with all of the lessons learned. Engineer4 was ready to meet someone. He didn't want to be on-line for an extended period. He really believed that he could find his "Mrs. Right" quickly and thus would not need to be online for a long time.

We decided to meet on a Wednesday evening after work. Where else would we meet but Rosie's Cantina, where you can have the best margarita in the world? When I arrived, he was already seated in the bar at a booth. I walked in and sat down across from him. My first impression: "Man he looks old and a little feminine!"

I sat across from him and listened to him talk about his children and his home and how lonely he was. Suddenly, his age or his feminine disposition did not matter. There was something about him that I really liked. His laugh, maybe. His voice? He was calm and humble. Maybe it was just the aura of peace around him. I am not quite sure, but he was really a nice man. "Let's go for a ride to the park and sit and talk," he said. And I agreed.

It was a beautiful night in Huntsville, Alabama. A light, spring evening. The perfect temperature for a nice walk in the park. So we exited the restaurant and walked to his car. He had a beautiful, white Nissan 380Z. Awwwww, sweet! I got into the car and he began to drive. The park was only a few miles away. During the drive, there was only enough time for a short conversation between us. There was time enough for him to brief me on HIS on-line dating experiences.

"I really thought that I would only be on-line for a weekend," he began, "but I went out with one lady on Monday night. She was really sweet. I would not mind seeing her again. Then last night I went out with another lady and we had a pretty good time too. Now, tonight, I have met you, and you are pretty fun as well." He paused for a moment and then went on… "I really thought that I would meet one person and she would simply shine above everyone else, but that didn't happen."

By this time, we had pulled up at the park. What was once going to be a nice, spring evening, ideal for a walk, was now something different. There was nothing nice about this night at all. "Take me back to my car," I said. With a confused look on his face, he replied, "WHY?" I looked over at him with every ounce of self-confidence that I could muster and I said, "Because I am going to be the one that shines!" (After all, I am Bamagirllluvsu – smiling).

I must say that Engineer4 was in a state of disbelief. He could not believe what he had just heard. "You are kidding me!" he said. "Really! Do you really believe that after one date I should know if you are going to be the one for me or not?"

"Not exactly!" I exclaimed. "I don't think you will KNOW that I am the ONE! But, I know that you will KNOW if I shine!" He drove me back to my car and I began to drive home.

I know what you must be thinking right now! How can I just leave this man that abruptly? How could I judge him this quickly for not simply falling for me? It's just this simple. I have been out with a lot of different men. And I know what I think immediately, right? I can judge. I can devalue. I can look for the negative. NOT! This is not usually what I do. Usually, I find all of the good in someone, before I will see any bad. I will overlook the fact that they are old-looking or feminine looking. After all, that part doesn't matter. It is the character. The personality. The depth of their heart. It is all of these more important things that matter anyway!

So why this time? Why did I judge Engineer4 so quickly? Am I beginning to learn that if it isn't there, you can't make it be? Am I maturing in my dating experiences? Am I becoming more confident in who I am, knowing that if I don't "shine" to this guy, then maybe I will shine with the next one? Have I finally reached the point that I quit looking for what isn't there? I have learned to accept things for what they are instead of trying to read between the lines and make something out of nothing! Yea me! (I am listening to the wind chimes that Bernie gave me as I write this and I am taken back to a point in time when I met a beautiful man that I didn't have to pretend with. I didn't have to search for something that wasn't there. Bernie just loved me for who I am. That is what I am looking for again and I won't stop until I find it)!

So, I am driving down the interstate and I think to myself, "It's early. Why should I go home? There is another man on-line that I have been chatting with, so why not call him? So... I DID!

School Teacher

"Tom, this is Sandy. Listen. I didn't have to work as late tonight as I thought I did. I am on the road driving home. Do you want to meet?" As I spoke these words to Tom, the school teacher that I met online, I am thinking to myself, "I hate lying! I am not good at it and I absolutely hate it! What are you doing, Sandy? What are you thinking? You are meeting two men in one night! This is terrible! You are a horrible, horrible person! No....No....No, you aren't. You haven't done anything wrong! It didn't work out with Engineer4, so why not meet someone new? This is okay! You are okay! It's the lying. The lying part that is so hard!"

Tom was thrilled to hear from me! "Absolutely! I would love to meet you!" he said. I met him at a bar and had a margarita. It was a small, quaint bar, and being Wednesday night, there were very few people there. It was a nice place for us to talk and get to know each other. My first impression of Tom was simple. He had dark hair and dark eyes. He seemed to be exciting and fun! Listening to him tell about his life and his hobbies captivated me. He was a school teacher. Yeah...and...what's so exciting about that? Well, he was also in a band. And he could sing. And he was passionate about it. He was actually doing the DJ'ing for a prom on Friday night and asked me to go.

Suddenly, I felt young again. I felt like a school girl, being asked to the senior prom again. My schedule wouldn't allow me to go, but it was still exciting to be asked. My mind raced with thoughts of this man and how exciting it would be to get in my red camaro and drive to whatever venue he would be playing at and be the "lady" in the audience that belonged to him. My imagination ran wild as I fantasized about being "his" girl.

I drove home that evening knowing that I would see this man again. He was intriguing and captivating. And he offered a life that was not dull. I could go to the prom again! Smiling.

As we go through life and technology changes, sometimes it is hard to change as quickly as the technology. Cell phones are great! They offer us an opportunity to communicate…to stay in touch. Tom sent me a picture of his daughter. A beautiful girl. The caption on the picture… "Isn't she beautiful?" I replied, "Of course she is…she is absolutely beautiful!" Then a second text arrives…from a different telephone number that states, "She is really beautiful!"

I replied back, "Why are you texting me from a different number?" His reply was… "What other number am I texting you from?" I sent Tom's "other" number to this "new" number. The reply: "This is Christine, Tom's other 'friend.' I think he sent both of us the same picture! LOL"

Okay. So modern day technology is great! Tom had sent the same picture to multiple "friends" which started a chat session. This would mean that any reply to this message would be seen by all recipients of the original message. Some of us in this modern day technology world are technologically challenged. We don't know everything that there is to know about the devices that we use, which makes us dangerous.

I sent a text to Tom. "Tom, you sent your previous text to multiple people, so I just had an interesting chat with your friend, Christine." I explained to Tom what had happened, thinking that this was pretty funny. This sounded like something that I would do. Literally. And I was literally laughing out loud (LLOL). Tom, on the other hand was not happy at all. He took offense to my text and replied back, "Sandy, I don't owe you anything. We just met!"

Wow! Really, Tom? I was kidding about the entire thing. I guess this man is out of my life too! There are a million men on-line... and I still have difficulty finding just ONE! But on this one night, I found TWO! I gave an entirely new meeting to the term, "DOUBLE DATE!"

♥♥The Blast from the Past♥♥

Sometimes, out of no-where comes the "blast from the past." You know what I am talking about. You can be going along in your life, having fun, not worrying about anything, and there he is. The one guy that you believed you fell in love with years ago. The one that broke your heart.

I was driving home from work one day, when I received a text from BFP (Blast from the Past), I shall call him "BP" for short. BP was the guy that I met for a brief time, ten years earlier, one of those "fix-ups" by a mutual friend. It was a Wednesday night and it was ladies night at a local bar. And of course, the men came in to scope the crowd. One of my friends called me over to meet BP. "Sandy," she said, "This is BP and I think the two of you should dance."

Of course, we did. Once our eyes met, it was over. We were both hooked. But what connected us the most wasn't physical at all. It was an emotional connection…a personality connection like I had never experienced before. We were laughing with each other and talking, finishing each other sentences. This was very rare for me. Here in small-town USA, I have achieved success in my career, and some men are intimidated by that success. This has made it difficult to meet men and relate. But I connected instantly and related to this man. And it was GREAT!

I shall not go too deeply into the ins and outs of this past relationship… WAIT! What relationship? That's just it. We never had an opportunity to date. We talked every night on the telephone. We laughed. He was such a jokester. It was great to be able to laugh with someone. We actually planned a real date. ONCE! And then…

BP was still in love with his ex-wife. He was recently divorced, and as most of us do, we want everyone to believe that we are over that other person. After all, we are divorced for a reason, right? So, why should the "EX" mean anything to us at all anymore? The problem for a lot of us in this world is that we didn't want the divorce. We wanted to be married to that person. We loved them. They were our life. It was the other person that decided they didn't want us anymore. This hurt and it hurt deep. A heartache. A heart-break... caused by unrequited love is damaging, especially when that person loved us at one time. But, something changed...with them...with us... What once was an incredible love became the thing that hurt us the most.

So BP was in this situation. He was out here in the single world again at no choice of his own. And he wanted me to believe that he was searching for his partner and friend, just as I was. Only, in his mind (and in his heart), his real partner and friend was still in control of his heart. So, even though BP and I had this phenomenal personality connection, that was truly all it was and all it ever would be. I just didn't know that at the time. So, I allowed myself to feel connected to this man, on a deeper level.

So that "almost date" that we NEVER had, was brought to an end by "Satan." That is what BP called his ex-wife. "Satan." There was no other name for her. He even had a black widow spider tattooed on his wedding finger as a symbol of what she had done to him and to remind him to never allow that to happen again. "Satan" decided that she didn't love BP, but as the old cliché goes, she didn't want anyone else to have him either. So she did everything she could to see to it that we didn't get together. She threatened me. She threatened to beat me up. She threatened to break every window in the house. She truly was "Satan"...or Mrs. Satan. Smiling again.

I ended the "almost" relationship pretty quickly with BP. I had very small children at home and this drama had turned into way more than I could handle. So just like that! What never started…was OVER.

BP and I remained friends over the years. He even came to my home once (before I married my last husband) and brought a card of apology. He wanted a chance to try again. He knew he had messed up by not letting go of his emotional attachment with his ex-wife, and he wanted to make things right with me. By this time, I had met my next ex-husband and was committed. I could not go back. So I moved on…into HELL with Satan himself, as BP left Satan's wife behind. Funny, how the world works, isn't it?

During the ten-year period that followed, I married. BP married and moved out of state. And we somehow managed to stay in touch with each other. On various occasions, we talked on the telephone, mostly small-talk, just checking in to see how things were going for each other. We never ended a telephone call without saying, "If you and I had just gotten together, we wouldn't be where we are today. We should be together." We would both laugh, as we recalled that instant connection that we had on that one Wednesday night so long ago.

So, driving home from work on this evening, I received the text from BP. "Hey, I'm single again, if you are single again. I think we should give this thing a shot. We never had a chance years ago, but now we do. What do you say?"

BP's text did not deserve a response with a text. It deserved a telephone call. A voice. From the heart. So, I picked up the phone and I called. "Well, BP," I said. "I have met this guy and we have only been out once or twice (the School Teacher), so the connection isn't there yet, so YES! YES, we should give this a try!"

BP was at his Mom and Dad's house that evening, caring for them. His dad had gotten sick and as many of you have had to do in later years, it became his turn to care for his dad. BP wanted to see me so he asked if I wanted to come over there. I drove to BP's family home, and walked inside. He gave me a huge hug and thanked me for coming. BP's dad was just as sweet and gentle as any old man would be. His mom was the typical southern hostess, trying to get me to eat something. I felt right at home.

His Dad had Alzheimer's, but he remembered me. "I remember you," he said. "You came to the hospital one time to see me." Wow! That was amazing that he remembered that. "I did." I replied. "I only stayed a minute, but I wanted to make sure you were okay." BP looked at me with astonishment. "You did? I never knew that!" I looked back at him and smiled. It was a great bonding moment for us.

I shall fast-forward to the reason that BP made it into the story of Bamagirlluvsu. BP shared a story with me about a friend of his. I shall call his friend Marcus. Marcus had a girlfriend, and I shall call her Betty. Betty had been diagnosed with lung cancer and had been given less than six months to live. One of the things that Betty wanted to do before she died, one of her bucket list items, was to go to the Thunder Beach Biker Rally in Panama City Beach, Florida. BP and Marcus had planned this trip with another couple and the guy lost his job. The trip was now off. BP was really saddened by the cancellation of this bucket-list trip for Betty. He really wanted to make this happen for her.

Anyone that knows Bamagirlluvsu would tell you that this was all it took for her. She immediately went online to VRBO.com© and began to search for a reasonably priced condo in Panama City Beach for the biker rally. Yes, I searched. I would have done anything to make this trip happen. So, I searched for hours until I found the perfect condo at the perfect price. It was a four bedroom/three bathroom condo and it was located right in the middle of it all. Right in the heart of Panama City Beach, Florida. And the rate was very reasonable. Everyone could now afford to go. UNTIL…. (Why does there always have to be an "Until…")?

BP called me in a panic. "Sandy, something has come up and now I don't have the money to go to Panama City." Of course we had to go! There simply was no other choice. "BP, don't worry about it." I said knowing that was all I could say. "I will pay for this. We can't let Betty down. She may not be around much longer."

The next day, the boys got on their bikes and the girls got in the red camaro and we headed to Panama City Beach, Florida. Meeting Betty was not what I expected at all. I anticipated a frail, weak woman with not much hope or faith in life. Instead, I met a vibrant, beautiful woman who smiled and laughed like she had the whole world ahead of her. She was truly amazing. I was inspired.

People come into our lives for a reason. BP and I broke up as soon as we returned from the Beach. He didn't have the same feelings that we had experienced ten years earlier. But, I know this about the trip to Panama City. Spending those four days with this dying woman had a profound effect on my outlook on life. I know that I already take one day at a time and I live life as fully as I can, but what I learned from Betty that week was how I took for granted each and every one of those days. I didn't fully appreciate each day for what it was…a gift from God. Each day that we wake up, it is a true gift. A gift of time… A gift of love… A gift of family… A gift of hope… and a gift of faith.

It has been four months since that trip to the beach and since I have heard from BP. Betty is now resting on that beach in the beautiful heavens above, looking down on us with a big smile. She knew my heart that week, and she continued to stay in touch with me as if she had known me for years. God does have a way of bringing the right people into our lives at the RIGHT time.

BFP (Blast from the Past)... Thanks for giving us the chance that we never had. Without this chance, I would have missed a really big opportunity. An opportunity to learn what it is to "live like you are dying." Rest in peace, my dear new friend. I love you, girl!

Song Application – "Live Like You Were Dying" – Tim McGraw©

♥♥The Baby Daddy♥♥

Time out! I am tired. This man-hunt had just about gotten the best of me. I didn't think I could do this anymore. After all of the driving and effort that I had put into this search, I had really gotten tired. I had also been involved in my stressful time at work and had worked extensive hours. I simply needed a break. It was a time for me to focus on me!

I was at my "Cheers" hanging out, drinking a few margaritas, singing, and dancing. Doing what I do. Hanging with friends. I was simply having a good, relaxing time. Jamie, my FSM, called me over to the table. "Do you see that table of guys over there?" she said. "All four of them are single." I looked over at the table at the four guys and checked each of them out. "I only know one of them," she said, "the one in the blue shirt. His name is Jamie too." I smiled. "Do you want me to introduce you?" she asked. "I got this." I said with the air of confidence that only Bamagirlluvsu could have. I walked toward the table.

"Hey guys. How are you doing this evening?" I asked as I stood between two of the guys, with Male Jamie to my left. (Yes, I eventually had to call them Male Jamie and Female Jamie. I couldn't keep up, otherwise). Then, I had the best "come-on" line of them all. I had no fore-thought about it. It just came to me. "I'm not getting those texts you are sending me," I said to Jamie. He looked at me and smiled. "I am not sending you texts," he said, "but I would if I had your number."

At least this wasn't one of the traditional come-on lines. It was different. Modern. And it broke the ice for us. We hung out that evening. Dancing. He was full of energy. And this man could really dance. I felt sexy dancing with him. There was just something about the way our bodies moved together. I had only seen this once in my lifetime. A friend from the past with her boyfriend could dance like no-one I had ever seen before. So, that is what I imagined in my mind. Jamie and I were dancing just like that. And it was great!

I laughed as I talked about it with my FSM's. "I know we look good dancing together," I said. "I can visualize it in my mind. The way we move together has to be the most sensual thing that you have ever seen." Female Jamie replied, "Sandy, I can video you the next time you are dancing and that way you can see what you look like."

"NO! NO!" I exclaimed. "You can't do that! You must not video us. I have this vision in my mind about what we look like and seeing it in reality might just ruin that for me! I want to keep this vision. We look good! We look sexy! I feel sexy and sensual. I DO NOT want to see a video and ruin all of those thoughts! We may never be able to dance together again!"

Song Application – "Country Girl, Shake it for Me" – Luke Bryan©

We laughed about it. Male Jamie and I had many more opportunities to dance together. I kept the vision and the internal excitement alive in my mind. I really liked this man! He was much younger than me. He was thirty-five and I was forty-nine, that is fourteen years! Fourteen years! I can't do this! That is too much! I had said I would go ten years younger, but not fourteen. This was breaking my own rules!

Jamie looked older than thirty-five. He had worked hard during his lifetime, and the wrinkles in his forehead were earned. And, of course, in spite of the hard life I had encountered, the aging process had been good to me. I was blessed that I looked younger than forty-nine (at least that is what everyone told me and I believed them)! I was still concerned about the age difference. I wasn't concerned about what people would think because I believed we didn't "look" the part. With him looking older and me looking younger, that meant we were closer in age than everyone knew. So, I wasn't concerned with what others thought. I was concerned with what was going to happen ten years down the road. I knew that life had been good to me so far, but what if I wasn't blessed to age gracefully in the years to come. Ten years from now, when I am fifty-nine and he is forty-five, then what? I questioned Jamie multiple times about this. "What will you do later down the road, when I age and I am not as youthful looking as I am now?" Jamie's response was, "Loving you will make the age difference irrelevant." Wow! Yes, he knew what to say. So I began to believe it myself! Age really doesn't matter.

It would matter if he had no children or wanted more children. My reproductive days had come to an end. I have three children and that was enough for me. Jamie had one son and he was seven years old. And Jamie was okay with having no more children. So, again, all the reasons that age should matter did not exist. So I was okay with Jamie. Why shouldn't I be? This was way too easy! And the dancing made it really fun!

My FSM's began to joke me about this. In this day and time, the era of the cougar and the MILF had evolved. (Do you know what a MILF is? The acronym? I had to ask someone because I did not figure out the meaning on my own. "MILF…Mother I would Love to F###" Wow, I had no clue). The cougar! I could not be a cougar! And I was not a MILF! What are these exactly? What does the age difference have to be for either of these labels to apply? I Googled© of course. Of course I did. I am the queen! There were varying definitions on the internet. So in one person's eyes, I could be a cougar or a MILF. And in another person's eyes, I would be neither. So, I just decided, again, that I didn't care. If it didn't matter to Jamie, then it wouldn't matter to me.

Jamie's financial struggles were tough. He worked hard and had the work ethic that he needed to succeed. He had ambition. And he had drive. He simply had not experienced luck or opportunity. But, he didn't let that stand in the way of meeting people or being happy. He didn't allow the fact that he had to struggle through life to pay his bills keep him from standing firm in the things that he believed in. He wanted me because I made him believe in himself again. I gave him the courage and strength to know that he wanted more for his son. He wanted to achieve more from life than what he had achieved thus far.

Jamie was a construction worker. Building houses. And I saw some of his work. The man was really good at what he did! So, I began to "build" him up. I began to give him a reason to excel and to perhaps go into business for himself. Be entrepreneurial. Be all that you can be. We are all given opportunity to excel beyond our current situation. It simply takes believing that you can exceed your own expectations (or at times the expectations of others, for sometimes we become what others expect us to become). You have to convince yourself that you are worthy and capable of so much more. I gave Jamie that new insight. Jamie began to talk about what he could do. He wanted to gain a new respect from his son so that his child would believe that his Dad was more and then he would want to be more.

The more you get to know someone, the more you get to know them. Wow! That is an eye-opener, huh? Well, let's say this. I recognized that Jamie was having a difficult time with money. But don't we all? I was raising three children and doing the best I could as well. There were times when I didn't know if I was going to make it to the next pay day or not. That is the nature of the economics of the world we live in today. So, when I began to cook dinner every night and to pay for everything that we did, I began to get a little resentful.

Resentful. Yet, okay. See, that is who I am. I always want to be the person that helps everyone else. I want to give all I can. It's not that I do it for praise or recognition. That is not it at all. I just have this internal drive or desire to make everyone happy. While this could be a good thing, it doesn't always work out for the good. Once others begin to learn this about you, they know they can use you for what you are worth. And your worth goes far beyond what can be measured in dollars and cents. It goes into what can be measured in time and energy. Sometimes we give more than we can give of ourselves. And it exhausts us.

I tend to allow others to drain me of everything that I can give. Not because it is apparent or obvious that this is taking place. It isn't. It is quite the opposite. Because this is the part of me that makes me who I am, it is a seamless opportunity. It just happens within me. Then I reach the point that I am exhausted. Drained. And I explode. All of a sudden, what once was okay is not okay anymore. I feel taken advantage of and used. I am a genuine giver. The problem is, in this life, there are a LOT more takers than givers. If you allow, others will take all of you- emotionally, physically, financially... You have to reach a point to give only when you WANT to. Then your motive is pure and it is true GIVING. Otherwise, it is not you giving, it is them TAKING! A BIG Difference!©

So that is exactly what happened one evening with Jamie and me. He was coming over and we began to talk about dinner plans. Understand. I had cooked a lot of meals for us. So, I decided to throw it out there. After all, we were new and dating. He should WANT to take me out. I was getting a little frustrated. Not knowing the entirety of his financial situation, I came out and asked, "Why don't you ever offer to take me to dinner?"

A discussion resulted in which I soon discovered that Jamie was having more than just day to day financial difficulty. At this point in time, I felt guilty. I felt really bad for bringing this up. So, I began to do what I do to save the day. "Forget I said anything. I didn't know the complete story. I am sorry. I am so sorry." We should now be okay. Life pursued onward. And I still thought Jamie was everything. After all, I could still feel the excitement and passion when we danced!

Song Application – "The Dance" – Garth Brooks©

The Bucket List

Go Braves! Can you believe that Jamie had never seen an Atlanta Braves game? There was so much that this man had never gotten to experience in his life, including going to Gulf Shores. This was the beach that has become the vacation spot for all of us here in Alabama and Jamie had never been. And the Braves? He had never seen them play either and he was a huge fan! It was very common for him to have his cell phone on the Braves application, tracking the games.

Belinda, my sister, had perks with her job. One of those perks was to get free tickets to sporting events. And she came through often with these free tickets, especially if it meant bringing joy to someone. When I called Belinda and asked if I could bring Jamie and his son, along with Izzy, to her house for a long weekend, of course she said yes. Her home had become known as the local "Bed and Breakfast". She always had her home available to family and friends. So the trip was planned and Braves tickets were ready.

Going to Atlanta with Jamie and his son was exciting. The weekend before the game, we took the boat out on Lake Lanier and Jamie's son had a blast. We drove the boat to a small island that also had a place you could get good "river food." We had burgers, pizza, fries, and nachos. You name it! We had it! There was also a splash pad. I took pictures of the little guy playing in the water. He had so much fun.

The Braves game was just as much fun to the young man, as well as his dad. Before the game, we went to the "Varsity" and had hotdogs. Sitting at the Varsity, Jamie commented that he was proud to be marking something off of his "bucket list." His son asked, "What's a bucket list?" I explained to him what a bucket list was. The sweetness in his voice, along with the excitement, stole my heart. "Dad....Dad..." he said. "I have to make a bucket list. I have to make a bucket list and put the Atlanta Braves game at the very top so that I can mark it off." I still tear up when I think of this. It really humbled my heart to know that I was contributing to the joy of this young man's life. I provided him the opportunity to create a bucket list and mark his first item off the list. SWEET!

When we returned home from Atlanta, I took the pictures that I had made and created the son a little "bucket list" book. There were pictures of him and his Dad at the game. They were granted the opportunity to mark a bucket list item off their list at the same time. The joy in his eyes when I gave him the book was priceless. He could not wait to get home and show this book to his Mom. Again...Sweet!

Your Best Friend Loves Me

Jamie's best friend was a friend for life. Literally. He had been friends with this guy since grammar school. So when Jamie told me that his best friend did not like his last girl friend nor did he like his ex-wife, I began to see a pattern. A pattern that it didn't matter who Jamie dated, his friend wasn't going to like her. But, I was determined that he would like me! After all, I am Bamagirlluvsu and that was enough!

129

His friend had a cookout at his house and I was invited. I made it a point to talk to his friend. I was going to be the girlfriend that he loved. I had to be. After all, I was crazy about Jamie so his friend had to be crazy about me. And he was. The problem: I am a friendly girl. I talk freely and openly. I can relate to all kinds of people. The rich. The poor. I can talk the talk of the intellectual or I can talk the talk of the typical southern redneck. I was born a poor, southern girl and grew up that way. I have been blessed to complete my education and work among professionals. I have continued in increasing my knowledge through continuing education classes and studying. So I have the gift of "gab" and I know how and when to use it.

So, when I met Jamie's best friend, it was easy for me to talk to him. And that is exactly what we did. Now, understand this. It wasn't that "the friend" and I were sitting around, just the two of us talking. You must see the big picture of it all. It was the Fourth of July. It was hot! There were about twenty adults and ten children sitting outside talking. We were all having a few drinks. Music was blasting. Food was cooking. It was a good day. I was sitting in a chair and "the friend" was standing up cooking. We were carrying on a conversation about life! When suddenly, the man says to me, "...little rich girl!"

What! Really? Did he just call me a little rich girl? Yes. He did! And he hit a nerve with me. I, by no means was rich. I was not poor, but I definitely was not rich. I totally get that the term "rich" is a relative one, just like the word, "poor" is as well. What is deemed as "rich" by one person isn't necessarily "rich" in another one's eyes. But, I felt the need to set this man straight. It was the connotation in which he used the words. It was the tone in his voice. Like he was demeaning me. I must say what I could to defend myself.

I pointed my finger at him, like we do here in the south as if it takes that extra pointing of the finger to drive the idea home, and I began to speak…directly…and loudly… "Listen to me," I said, "I am not a little rich girl. You should get your facts straight before you go throwing out words. My parents had an eighth grade education. My mom was a waitress and my dad was a truck driver. They divorced when I was six years old. We grew up with NOTHING! Both parents died when I was younger and I struggled to pay my way through college. Everything that I have is because I worked my tail off to get here. Get your facts straight about people before you start saying what you think!"

The look on his face said it all. He had been set straight and everyone knew it. Everyone, including Jamie. Everyone, including his wife. The man began to stutter and stammer as he mustered up the best apology that he could. "I am so sorry," he said. "I really am sorry." He continued on and on. I told him it was okay. I just did not want anyone to believe that I was born with a silver spoon in my mouth. And I was not rich. I was battling pay day to pay day just like the rest of the group present that day. It was the appearance I gave. After all, Bamagirlluvsu does drive the hot, red camaro. I guess that provided an assumption and presumption of certain other things. It's okay. I set him straight. All in the world was good!

Absolutely not!

As the cookout went on, I began to do what I do best. Be me. Loving. Caring. The children there loved me because I gave them attention that sometimes children don't receive. There was a young teenage boy present. And this young man, like so many other teenagers, really enjoyed the hard rock/rap music. He made a statement about the country music on the radio, and I looked at him and said, "I understand what you mean, I kinda like the other stuff better myself." My daughter has started listening to this stuff on the radio, and it is growing on me. He wanted me to come into the house and listen to some of the music that he liked. He made several trips outside to remind me of the CD's he had and finally I went inside. This young man began to play some music that he just knew I would love. As I stood there listening to songs I had never heard before, I made this young man feel that he was worthy of something. He began to open up to me about his life. I took an opportunity to talk to this young man about the negative connotation associated with rap music and drugs and spoke to him about the negative influence that drugs can have on one's life. I gave him my telephone number and told him if he ever needed anything to be sure to call me. I felt like I was where I was supposed to be at that moment. You never know when you are granted an opportunity like that, what part of your words might sink in and come back to the forefront of someone's mind one day.

There was also a young girl present at the party. She was about six years old. She began to talk to me. Laugh with me. She wanted attention and I gave it to her. I went to my car and gave her some lip gloss. She loved it! After that, she wanted to hang out with me the rest of the day. She even wanted to ride with me to the store later. There was an instant connection to me. It is what I do. I care.

The "best friend's" wife also wanted to talk. She had changed clothes and put on a mini skirt and new top. She came outside in front of her husband and asked, "What do you think, Sandy? Do you like my skirt? Do you like my new top?" I told her she looked great! When she left, her husband looked at me and asked, "What was that all about?" I replied, "I don't know. She wasn't trying to find out what I thought. She doesn't know me. I think she really was trying to get your attention. I think she really wanted to know what you thought."

I am telling all of this to set the foundation for what was about to happen next. I am a flighty person. If there is a big crowd of people, I will run from one person to the next. Talking. Laughing. Just having a good time. I enjoy people. And I am a hugger. I love to express my internal feelings or love for people. So, when Jamie called me to the car to "talk", I actually had no clue what was coming next.

"Sandy," he said. "We need to leave. Apparently, you have made 'best friend's'wife jealous. She thinks that you are coming on to her husband and she is really jealous." This hurt my feelings. Really bad. I had NEVER tried to come onto this man. After all, there were only thirty people present, including kids. If I were going to come onto someone, it would not be in a crowd of people where everyone could see! Really! Who thinks this way?

And so it began to be discussed that I touched "best friend" on the shoulder. Really? OMG, shoot me now! "I can certainly see why everyone would be so upset," I thought to myself sarcastically. That is such a terrible thing! I touched him on the shoulder! This was almost too much for me. A part of me wanted to laugh. Then a part of me was upset. I could not believe that everyone was taking this so personally.

Jamie and I left that day. We went back to his house to talk. The "best friend" called him to find out what was going on. The friend wasn't aware that anything had happened. He could not understand why we had to leave. Jamie explained to him what had happened with his wife. The "best friend" explained to Jamie that I did not come onto him. I told Jamie that I could not understand what was happening. I said I didn't come onto his best friend. And the best friend said I didn't come onto him. So where is the problem? What did I do? ABSOLUTELY NOTHING!

The Baby Mama Drama

I guess you are all wondering where the title of this chapter came into play? "The Baby Daddy"… Well, here goes! MORE DRAMA!

When I first met Jamie, we were sitting in the living room on the couch and I asked a very important question. "When was your last relationship?" This is an important question. You must know how old or new the relationship is, to know if there are possible feelings that could still exist. Is there a chance that you could be giving your heart to someone while their heart still belongs to someone else? The expression in Jamie's eyes indicated something wasn't quite right. He didn't have to respond. No answer was necessary. I knew instantly. I looked at him and said, "She is pregnant, isn't she?"

"How did you know?" he asked. Somehow I just knew. I don't know how I knew, I just did. Jamie continued to explain that he had discovered the girlfriend was texting another man. Sex-texting (This was the first time I had ever heard this term). So, they had broken up. Bamagirlluvsu became the girl that wants to take care of everyone. I looked at Jamie and said, "It's okay. I will stand by you, no matter what." And I meant it. I would stand beside him. No matter what!

Looking back in time, I wonder why I even came up with that statement. How did I ever agree to that? All of my children were older! Would I really consider raising a baby from birth? At the time, it just seemed like the right thing to do…the right thing to say. It was what was expected of me, I guess. I liked Jamie and he needed me in his life. And it felt really good to be needed.

After the incident with the best friend, Jamie and I attempted to continue with our relationship. But everything that had occurred with the best friend and with the due date of the baby getting closer and closer, there was a lot of stress falling on us. We were getting a little touchy about things. Everything that we said or did seemed to cause an argument. I hated this. All of it! What once was easy had now become hard.

It wasn't long until Jamie told me that he couldn't handle it anymore. It was time for him to go on his way. We weren't going to make it. I was making him feel inferior…like he wasn't good enough for me. Wow! This was never my intent. I truly just wanted to do the right thing. I truly just wanted to help.

After Jamie began his new life without me, I continued to touch base with him. I could not understand how he could just walk out on something that began so easy. He finally confessed that he did not have a choice. His ex-girlfriend called him and told him if he didn't stop seeing me that he would not be allowed to see the baby. Life just really sucks sometimes! I felt so badly for him. He was one of the few men that wanted to stand up and be responsible for the child that he created. It wasn't fair that bribery was involved. It wasn't fair to him at all. But at least he was trying to do the right thing.

I realized later that there was a possibility that Jamie really may have cared about the ex-girlfriend. Maybe it wasn't all about him doing right by the baby. Maybe he really wanted to still be in the baby's mama's life as well. And, maybe just maybe, Jamie has as much difficulty with hurting others as I do. Either way, I was out of his life and he was out of mine.

Looking back. This is what is best. Jamie is busy being the "Baby Daddy" and I am moving on to find my Mr. Right. There really was too much drama in what started out as a drama-free relationship. What was I thinking? Dating the

"Baby Daddy" meant that I had to be a "Baby Mama" again! NO WAY!

♥♥Father of the Year♥♥

Knock Knock Knock! Let me in! I am back! I had decided I was tired. But now I am back. Fishing again. There are only a million men in this world. I only want one of them. Just one! The right one, but just one!

I was in my woman cave. Relaxing. Laptop in hand. I pulled up my profile and began to browse. I was window-shopping, when suddenly, there appeared a new man. This man appeared to be different. He was attractive as many of the others had been, but there was more to this man than met the eye. I continued to look. All of his pictures were of him and his three children. There were no pictures of him and another woman…at all…ever…back for several years. Just him and his three beautiful children.

Reading his profile, I was captured instantly. Something grabbed me and pulled me into him. There it was…the statement that I have been looking for…and of course anyone can say the words. It takes a man of honor and pride to mean them. "I am looking for someone that will laugh with me and have fun with me. I am looking for honor and respect. I am looking for a real relationship. I DON'T SERIAL DATE!"

Okay, I have to admit it, I Googled©. I looked up what "serial dating" was. Knowing grammar and the meaning of most words, I could kinda guess that it means dating one person after another, but exactly what does that really mean? When you are online searching, you can go out with one person and find that you really don't like them, so you move on to the next person. Isn't that really serial dating? Or does that mean you date someone for a while, then decide it isn't working out, so you move on to the next date? What exactly is serial dating?

Mr. Father of the Year and I began to chat online. We began to talk. A LOT. Every day. Every night. There was a real connection made as I began to listen to him talk about his children. I could hear the love for his children in his voice…in his words. One night, I sent him a friend request on Facebook© and he accepted. So, I began to review his Facebook© profile. Again, there were only pictures of him and his children.

Scanning through his pages, I found a link. There was a link to an on-line parenting blog. Of course, I clicked it. I was on the telephone with Mr. Father at this time. As I was chatting with him, I began to read the on-line blog. He had written a letter to his children. As I read the letter, I literally began to cry. His letter was written in terminology that the children could understand. It was a letter of apology and a letter of commitment at the same time. Wow! I must share this story.

He and the children's mother had gone through a divorce many years earlier. And the divorce was hard on everyone, especially the children. Coping… developing …moving on… sharing time… back and forth… All of these things that go along with divorce that makes it hard on the children. His children were faced with the same things. In a few short weeks after the divorce, which certainly was not enough time to get things straight in one's mind, Father of the Year received a telephone call. A horrible telephone call about the children's mother.

Mr. Father told me the rest of the story after I read his letter. His letter was so sweet and so genuine. He must let his children know how sorry he was for what happened to them. It wasn't just the divorce and having to adapt to the change. But it was the fact that now, they must know their Mom had just been killed in a terrible automobile accident.

WOW! Talking about a humbled heart. I reached out to this man. I hurt for him. I wanted to help him. What could I do? Sympathize. Empathize. How? I had lived through divorce (and sometimes, we all want to think that death would be easier), but I had lived through nothing like this man had lived through.

I began to express my thoughts of empathy with him. "I can't believe this. Life is so unfair. How can I even begin to understand what you went through? Divorce is tough enough. On you. The kids. But it is nothing like this. You never had a chance to grieve…to get angry…to go through all of the emotions that one goes through after a divorce. You had to immediately forgive, so that you could help your children."

He didn't have visitation in which every other weekend the children went away to Mom's house. He suddenly was a full-time single parent faced with raising three children by himself. He had parents, the children's grandparents, to help him. But, mostly, he was alone.

I heard conversations about how the children did not want their own room because they NEEDED each other. They wanted to all sleep in the same room so that they could feel the care and comfort of each other. This man later allowed the children to design and paint their own rooms as he helped them and posted pictures of them on Facebook©. I looked through the pictures and cried.

Bamagirlluvsu had met her match. This one was tough. This man had heart. He had forgiven his wife for the things she did to tear apart the family. He had to forgive her. He had to create fond memories for the children. (Okay, all of you divorcee's out there! You KNOW how hard this is to do! When a divorce is over, you are ANGRY!!!! And you want the world to KNOW. Think about this one with me, please)! This man talked about how he must allow the children to still love their mother. His letter to them, told about how he loved their mother. I was so touched by this man.

Father of the Year was a busy man. Between his job and his children, and his "parenting magazine," he had very little time for me. It wasn't like my situation in which the children go away to the other parent's house and I am allowed dating time and a chance to meet other people. His situation was totally different. He really was a single parent!

One evening, I was sitting home alone when I received the telephone call from the "Father of the Year." He wanted to meet me for a drink and see if we had an initial connection. The initial "meet and greet." Of course I wanted to go. This man had captured my heart. I had really placed him on a pedestal. He became the man that all men in my life had never been. I marveled at what this man had experienced in life and the way he so graciously handled it all. And I wanted to be a part of that life that he had created for himself. This was the man for me and I knew it!

I jumped into my red camaro and made another road trip. This trip was only 45 miles away, but still another road trip for Bamagirlluvsu. I was excited and elated. I was SOMEBODY and I KNEW it! No-one could take this feeling away from me! This man that I had built up so extremely in my mind, allowed me to reverse the feelings and impose them upon myself. If this man could want me, then that had to mean that I was worthy!

I made the trip to Decatur, Alabama that day. I met the Father of the Year. And I soon discovered what "serial dating" really meant. Mr. "Father of the Year" did not consider himself a serial dater because he never really dated at all. He had created a life for himself with his children and he never wanted another woman to be a part of that life. We met. I returned home to my world. He returned to his. I was given the explanation that he didn't really want a relationship right now, and he moved on to the next person that he wasn't going to "serial date."

Looking back, I guess I can see now that he just "wasn't that into me." But, at the time, I wanted it so badly, that I thought I would never want to date again. This one depressed me. This one brought me down. This one sent me home to my "woman cave" in which I crawled into my bed and never wanted to crawl out again. This man, because I had him on such a pedestal, brought me to my knees.

Song Application – "I'm a Survivor" – Reba McEntire©

How can anyone put that much faith and hope into a human being? This man really was "all that" in my eyes. Anger set in for me. However, anger is simply a by-product of fear. It is what we fear that makes us angry. My fear: that I would never meet a man that I felt was worthy of me…or to say it more truthfully…that I would never meet a man of character that believed I was worthy of him. I had to send the "Father of the Year" one last and final message to get my point across. The message read: "So, Mr. Father of the Year, are you busy going from town to town, meeting all of the single mothers of the world and making them feel special, just to let them down? Why don't you write a story about that for your parenting magazine?!"

This time, I was ignored…blocked…sent away to cyber-space…And I deserved it!

Mr. Father of the Year could do no wrong in my eyes. He was a grand provider and father. And perhaps, he never allowed himself to love again. His mission in life was to be the best father…the best parent that he could be and no-one can shame him for that. We all have that goal. I hope that he is happy and commend him for the unselfish efforts that he is making for his children, as he pushes forward to fill the role of two parents. Life is hard.

♥♥The Black Jack Player♥♥

Okay. So, I didn't stay down long. Yes, I crawled into my bed and wallowed in my own self-pity as if the "Father of the Year" was the only man in this world. But then...I got my butt out of bed and got on with my life. Bamagirlluvsu doesn't stay down long!

Song Application - "I Get Knocked Down, But I Get Up Again" - Chumbawamba©

On-line again. Fishing again. Searching again. I decided to try Chattanooga, Tennessee this time. Maybe someone different would appear. Chattanooga was about ninety miles from Huntsville. This would not be much further than my existing drive. So, I began my browsing.

There appeared a beautiful man with a young child on a riding lawn mower. My first thoughts were "What a sweet man to be riding his grandson around on the lawnmower." I later learned that he had two very young children, ages one and three. (This was another one of the men that I had to look back on later and ask myself, "What were you thinking?)!!!

What captured my eye? His profile! Yes, this time it was the words...not the pictures. I know that we are all visual people, but this time, my eyes were captured by the beautiful way he worded his profile. "I am seeking someone that has a strong commitment to family, outgoing personality, a good MOM or a MOM in the making, to all kids, makes plans around the kids and not plan the kids around themselves, understands busy work schedules, INTELLIGENT, thinker, and mostly, is organized."

WOW!

Let's move on:

"Let's be clear. If your photos are misrepresented (thin or thick), your current status is mis-stated (married, separated, single, divorced), height (short or tall), education (still working on, graduated), there is a good chance I will leave your a## sitting at the table or on the curb."

Okay, so let's just say that this man has seen the false advertisements as well. He is simply telling it like it is! If you are going to lie about who you are, then he doesn't want you to even make an effort of outreach to him. GREAT! I LIKE IT!

More directness: "Finally, I don't have the time nor do I want to take the time figuring things out messaging and texting back and forth, soon after we exchange a few communications, let's try to connect." Yes, he said it. Just like I always had said it. You can sit behind a computer and chat with someone. You can talk on the telephone for days upon end. But you never know the real connection until you actually meet.

As I read this man's profile and discovered that he was in the finance industry as well, I realized that this was a fitting person for me to meet. We talked and chatted for those few days just as we all should. After all, we must give ourselves a chance for our intuition to kick in and speak to us. We must believe that the person we are going to meet is deemed safe. We have to give our inner voice the chance to speak. My inner voice had spoken and Bamagirlluvsu was ready for another ROAD TRIP!

The night before I was to make that drive to Chattanooga, Tennessee, I was chatting with "Blackjack Player" and he sent me a picture. I love receiving pictures from my potential dates. Pictures can say so much. You can never see too many pictures. What might not be evident in one picture may be evident in another. Pictures show us, not only what is obvious in the pictures: hair/physique, eyes, taste in clothing, etc. But, pictures also show us things that aren't meant to be so evident. In a picture, you can see what is in the background: the messy closet, the towels laying on the bathroom floor, the glass of wine on the counter, etc.

The picture that "Blackjack Player" sent me was of him in the shower. Wait…Wait…don't judge him, yet (or me…for looking). He was funny. He was tasteful…(well, as tasteful as you can be with this picture). This man was proud of his body and that was obvious. It would take a confident man to be able to take a nude picture of himself in the shower. He was tasteful enough, however, to hide his male extremities with a shampoo bottle. Yes, there he stood in the shower with the shampoo bottle in hand, hiding…

OR WAS IT HIDING??????

I looked and I looked closely. What? Did he really send me a picture of his male organ? Before he had even met me, he had actually had the nerve to send me this picture…

My thoughts: "Awwwww….I feel sorry for him…"

Then, I text back: "I can't believe you sent me this picture…"

His response: "It is hidden by the shampoo bottle."

I took a second look. I zoomed in. I zoomed a little more. I looked a little harder…a little deeper into the picture. Yes, he was correct. I believe. What's that? What was I seeing if it wasn't the part I thought I was seeing? His FOOT! Really? Was it his foot in the picture…a part of his foot. From the angle that the picture was taken, he had caught his big toe just at an angle that it appeared in the picture as his…

I had to call him after this. We laughed so hard. Without zooming, you would never see this for what it really was. I explained to him that I was feeling sorry for him there for a minute. Priceless comedy, with no effort at all.

21

The drive to Chattanooga, Tennessee wasn't a bad drive. It was quite a beautiful drive. The Blackjack Player had sent me his address. I programmed it into my GPS and I headed to his small home in Tennessee.

NOT! NO WAY! THE HOUSE WAS FAR FROM SMALL!

When I arrived at this man's home in Tennessee, I was overwhelmed. His home was phenomenal. And this was a starter home. He was only staying there a few years while his other home was being built. I walked in and we introduced ourselves. He took me through the house and showed me around. I was impressed beyond this Alabama girl's belief. The kitchen was incredible. There sitting in the middle of the kitchen on an island was every drink that I had ever mentioned liking. There were ingredients for the best margarita that you could create, buttery nipple shots, wine, etc. Anything I wanted, he was prepared to make.

But first, there must be a tour of the media room. Being from Alabama, a media room is of rare occurrence. This media room was a BAMA girl's dream. This was the perfect room for gathering to watch those BAMA football games (okay…okay…any sports game, but I have to get my next ROLL TIDE in). I have to say that I was definitely impressed. The television covered the entire length of the wall. There was seating that covered the entire room in a half-circular format with places to set those adult beverages. Yes, this was a BAMA girl's dream!

We returned to the kitchen, where we had a glass of wine. As I sat across from this man, I began to explain that his home was so far above what I had ever experienced in my life. I had to humbly admit that I was a small-town girl, and felt a little intimidated. "Blackjack Player" made it clear to me that I should not feel intimidated. He was a small-town guy himself. He had worked really hard to make it where he was. He began to tell me about his profession. He was also in the finance profession; however, his was in a "for profit" area. His profession entailed taking companies that were failing and turning them around. At times, he would save several companies at once by suggesting (or advising) that several companies join together to form a completely new profitable company. This conversation about our financial professions lasted for several hours, until the wine finally took over every intelligent thought that could occupy my brain.

As this conversation gradually ended, I noticed that the "Blackjack Player" was shuffling a deck of cards. "Do you know how to play poker?" he asked. "No, I said, but I can play blackjack."

"Blackjack it is." He said. "Strip Blackjack!"

"What? Really? Strip Blackjack! Uhhhhhhhhhh……" I stammered. "Wait, this isn't fair," I said as I looked down at the dress I was wearing. "First, I only have on A DRESS, which once removed will reveal my undies, and I did not anticipate this so I don't exactly have on my sexy undies. This really isn't fair."

"Okay," he said. "I will allow your jewelry to count." I looked down at my two bracelets and watch on my arm and felt a relief. I believed that I could win this, so I agreed.

With the wine now having settled in, my brain was spinning. I still knew enough about what was going on to count numbers in my head. After all, I am an accountant and I am a numbers fanatic. I can do this, I thought. This is how the blackjack tournament played out:

Hand One: I lost (bracelet removed).

Hand Two: I lost (bracelet removed).

Hand Three: He lost (shirt removed) – Okay, I must stop here and say that this man was really hot!!!!! Those abs rippled in front of me…And I still HAD to concentrate!

Hand Four: I lost (watch removed) – I was so thankful that the rules included jewelry. I would be naked by now. Whew!

Hand Five: He lost. He looked at me and said, "Okay, you win!"

"Really?" I questioned. "What about your underwear?" His reply, of course, "I don't have any on." I looked at him and smiled and said, "Say NO more!"

So did I win? Or did he win? I still had my dress and my undies on. I would say that I maintained as much grace and style as I could maintain, considering the body that lay beneath that shirt. Meeting the Blackjack Player was fun and intellectual. Being able to carry on a conversation with him about financial matters, including explaining how the Tax Credit program worked was intriguing for me. Listening to his business plan and learning the ways of his world was impressive.

Playing Blackjack and WINNING or LOSING! Priceless.

This was a one-time date with the Black-Jack player. Perhaps he was a sore loser because he wanted to reveal what was beneath the shampoo bottle. Maybe he felt the need to disprove my self-perceived notion about what was revealed by the camera snafu. Who knows? He got too busy working and raising babies to pursue a relationship or call me again. Such is life. Such is the nature of the game. Sometimes you win! Sometimes you lose! And sometimes…it's simply a PUSH!

♥♥Dirtbikerider♥♥

How many men have the guts or the confidence it takes to stand in front of the bathroom mirror and snap a picture of themselves? Not naked. No shirt. Pants slightly unbuttoned, lying just below the belly button, revealing the beautiful abdominal muscles above. NOT MANY!

But "Dirtbikerider" did. This man was a beautiful blonde and that was his profile picture. His profile: Age 45 (he was really 50), never married (mmmmm wonder what's wrong with him? Yes, we all ask that), blonde hair, blue eyes, and GORGEOUS! Wow!

I sent the first email. The first point of contact. I commented on his picture. And that I was attracted to his air of confidence. I expressed interest and waited. He responded with something like this: "Routinely, I don't respond to bigger girls, but you captured my attention. You have a beautiful smile and a beautiful face. With the right motivation, you could be a really attractive girl."

What! You have got to be kidding me! Seriously! Does this really work for this guy?

I replied, "Dear Sir: With no disrespect toward you at all, but I must ask, does this really work for you? Does this really win women over? Because I have to say this…I AM NOT FAT! LOL, Smiling." I added the LOL and Smiling so that he wouldn't believe I was really mad. But, I was pretty ticked. Why would anyone say that to someone they don't even know? Why did I continue talking to this guy?

Why? Because this is BAMAGIRLLUVSU and I must prove this man wrong! I must talk to him further to see what it is about him that makes him the judge of beauty in women. I must stay strong in my pride and belief that I am worthy. I am desirable. I am beautiful. I did not need his validation.

Then came the conversation about healthy weight. Dirtbikerider began to emphatically explain to me what the ideal weight was for someone my size. "The internet is deceiving," he said. You really can't look it up." Yes, I can.....I am the Google© queen!

And, of course I did. The ideal weight for someone five feet tall is 96 to 118 pounds (for a small frame). Then I emphasized the facts to Mr. DIRT, "Okay, Mr. Dirtbikerider, I am overweight, I agree. But I am only 15 pounds or so, and I can lose that much in a few weeks." Dirtbikerider replied, "You are wrong. Your ideal weight is 96 pounds. The high end is only put out there because of media perception. The medical industry has convinced everyone that it is okay to be at the high end of the scale. When it really isn't okay. If you want to get the good guys, the men on the high end of the measurement stick, you have to weigh 96 pounds."

I won't have to tell you that this conversation continued. I was not going to agree with him. So Bamagirlluvsu was convinced she had to meet this man. I had to allow him to see me. Once he saw me and placed the personality with the "beautiful smile and face," the rest would not matter. Why? Why on earth did I feel the need to convince this man that I was worthy? That I was beautiful on the inside and that my personality would accentuate my real beauty. Why? Because I am Bamagirlluvsu!

Squirter?

The next topic of conversation and a pretty embarrassing moment was this: I was looking through his profile, reviewing his likes, his hobbies. I was seeing the normal things. Racing. Going out to eat. Computers. Squirters. etc.

"Squirters," I thought. "What is a squirter?" Some of you reading this are going to be thinking to yourself right about now, "What an idiot!" Okay, go ahead and think it. I do live in small-town, Alabama, and I apologize in advance for not ever having heard of this term before. So, laugh at me, if you will, when I proceed to tell you how I asked Dirtbikerider about this term.

"Dirtbikerider, may I ask, what is a squirter? Is it a type of dirtbike?" (LOL...LOL...LOL...I know you are laughing. Go ahead. Get it out of your system). Yes, he responded. And he responded with all honesty that he could respond. "Sandy, really, are you asking me that? You really don't know?" As he said it, my mind began to wonder and I started to think to myself. "There is no way that it is what I am presuming that it is," I thought. But I would not dare ask. I continued to play stupid and questioned again, providing him the opportunity to tell me himself.

Squirter defined: "A squirter is a girl, that when the point of orgasm is reached through the manipulation of the G-spot, squirts a lot of fluid from her vagina." Okay, so maybe I tried to define it in classier terms and that might not be the exact words that he used, but you get the point. And of course...I...Googled!!!!© The pictures defined the word much better than words can define the word.

I would be lying if I said this conversation ended here. Because it did not. Dirtbikerider was proud to go on and explain further. You see, he had become the KING of stimulation. He could bring almost any woman to this point. He had gotten really good at this and it had been his experience from speaking to most women that other men don't take the time to learn a woman's body so that they can also develop this expertise. Mr. Dirtbikerider had taken women to this point of ecstasy that they had not ever achieved anywhere else. Therefore, they became stalkers. They wanted him. OVER and OVER and OVER. They became addicted to him or at least to the rewards that resulted from sleeping with him.

This has got to be the biggest and best (or worst) line I have heard. Was he being real? Could he really do this? I must say, if you have never reached this point of ecstasy and you hear someone tell you that they can take you there, it does spark your curiosity. So, yes I was curious. My mind had been captivated. I had seen the pictures on the internet. Yes, it crossed my mind….

BRIEFLY!

Then, we met. This man had my curiosity up and so I decided to at least meet him. I wanted to see if he truly was everything that he believed he was. I wanted to see what made him so special that he could judge my appearance and make such harsh statements about my outer beauty, when he didn't know my inner beauty. He didn't know me at all.

When he arrived at the restaurant, he came up to the table and sat across from me. The conversation went something like this:

His opening line was "I see you are drinking a margarita. You know that is why you are 40 pounds over-weight. Alcohol is a huge contributor to weight gain. And…I think you are an alcoholic. You drink more than you should!"

I looked at him and said, "Does this really work for you? Does this really get women for you? First of all, I am not 40 pounds over-weight. Second of all, I am not an alcoholic! YOU DON"T KNOW ME!" He proceeded to try to convince me that my ideal weight was really 96 pounds and for me to prove to him I wasn't an alcoholic by not drinking for 30 days.

I must say by this point I was feeling a little perturbed. Anger doesn't even begin to describe my internal abruption of fire. This man did not even know me and he was already passing judgment on me. I could not believe this. Why was I even here?

Song Application – "R-E-S-P-E-C-T" – Aretha Franklin©

I left the restaurant that day with the anger still spewing inside of me, thinking to myself about his "squirter" fetish and wishing I could have shown him the true definition of a "squirter." Squirter as defined by Bamagirlluvsu: "When a bama-girl's temperature is raised to its limit by a man who doesn't have a clue about women, so she "squirts" her FATTENING MARGARITA right in his DESERVING face!!!"

My phone was going crazy from texts as this man continued to send accusatory texts. I finally threatened to block him from my cell phone. His reply to that was that he worked in computers and he could get past the block. I was so crazy for ever meeting this man. No amount of squirting in this lifetime would be worth the ridicule this man would put me through. There is a little thing called intimacy. How could you even get close enough to this man to reach a level of intimacy that would even allow you to pursue anything sensual? NO WAY!

The squirting days were over even before they began! GOODBYE!

♥ ♥The Magic Mirror Man♥ ♥

Meeting people on-line is easy. Meeting the right person on-line…hard. I am soon discovering that it isn't any easier meeting someone online than it is in person. You can just meet a lot MORE of the WRONG people on line. On this day, I saw yet still another beautiful man on-line. His eyes, of course caught my eye. The first picture of him was distinguished. He had on a nice sports coat and the salt and pepper hair. Wow! My Richard Gere! Then he had a second picture of himself with darker hair (he probably colored it – don't we all do that at least once?) and dark sunglasses. This is the picture I like. This is the one that I hope he looks like now.

The Magic Mirror Man lived in Nashville, Tennessee. He was my age. I sent him an email:

"You need to put more in your profile. We women are open-minded and open-hearted! Wow! I love your pics!"

The Magic Mirror Man replied: "Hey, pretty lady! Wow, you like to write and you are good at it! Maybe you can help me with my profile!"

After that, I sent him a chat request. No response. So, I sent another email, telling him that I sent a chat request. This is when I found out that the Magic Mirror Man was new to the on-line dating world. He did not know how to do a chat. Not only would I need to help him write his profile, but I would also need to try to help him with chatting. After several tries, he and I could not connect with a chat session, so I trusted my gut instincts and sent him my telephone number.

The Magic Mirror Man called. I shall call him… "Richard" after Richard Gere. Yes, this man is my Richard Gere. He is incredibly beautiful!

Richard and I began to talk. I loved this man's accent. He was truly a southern gentleman. His laughter was "contagious." Do I dare use the same word to describe his laugh as others use to describe mine? I guess I will. His accent was more southern than my own. And I loved to hear him talk. It did not take us long to realize that there was a definite attraction and connection. Richard began to discuss wanting to meet. He liked me! He had been online only a few days at the advice of a friend. He had not dated anyone in a long time, but he liked me and wanted to meet me.

I asked him why me? "Richard, why do you want to date me when you haven't wanted to date anyone else?" His reply: "Because you get me, Sandy! You really get me!" Richard had a sarcastic sense of humor and it was prevalent throughout our conversations. He had such a way with words that it would make me laugh so hard. And vice versa. I also made him laugh. Yes, we truly "got" each other.

Richard was open and honest, just like me. His life was an open book. He began to tell me about his life. He owned a home in Nashville, where his children lived. He also had two farms, one in Kentucky and one in Oklahoma. The interesting part of his life: The Magic Mirror.

Richard was involved in a joint venture with a company in China called Coscar. This company had developed and created the "Magic Mirror." To listen to Richard describe the mirror was interesting to say the very least. This mirror is a virtual mirror, manipulated by a computer (as is everything else in this world today). It works with the same concept as an X-Box Kinect. You stand in front of the mirror and as you swipe your hands, something happens. This is how it works:

You go into a department store to try on clothes. We all know how tiring and sometimes disappointing this can be as we go through the store, picking and choosing what we want to try. We go into the dressing room trying on multiple outfits and varying sizes. And by the end of the session (several hours later), we are exhausted and humiliated....and we feel FAT! We all do! It is human nature! We have looked at ourselves in the mirror trying on varying outfits that looked great on the rack, but terrible on our not-so-perfect bodies. Along comes the Magic Mirror!

You step in front of the Magic Mirror, dressed. You don't have to take anything off...you don't have to go through the store shopping for varying outfits and accessories to match. Instead, you pre-select what you are looking to try on (or have someone else select for you), and you stand in front of the mirror and swipe your hand. Poof! In the reflection of the mirror, there you stand, fully clothed in your new outfit! You don't have to worry about what size you need. If you like the outfit, you mark it as a favorite and move to the next outfit! Swipe! Poof! Swipe! Poof! Over and over as you look at yourself in multiple outfits and you don't have to take any clothes off! You don't smear your makeup or mess up your hair. And you don't have to reveal the fat displayed by the nakedness of your body. Self-esteem just increased ten-fold!

You don't like the accessories – Swipe! Poof! A new purse, a new necklace, scarf, shoes...Swipe! Swipe! Poof! Poof! Wow, the Magic Mirror is incredible! Richard began to explain that these were still in the pilot stages and were being tested in three cities in the United States. I was so impressed with this story.

This man I had to Google©! He had definitely, magically pulled me into his world. When I Googled© him, there he appeared. He was on-line in several searches, one being the Better Business Bureau. And yes... there it was...his farms were online, along with the gross income for the prior year. Yes, modern day technology is great! He was so Googable!!!!! (Googable! Funny! A new word)!

Next...the "Magic Mirror." I had to google© the Magic Mirror! And there it was, a You-tube© video! So, I watched. There, on-line was a video illustrating the Magic Mirror and how it worked. Truly, I knew that the video could not do the magic of the mirror justice. This was something that you would definitely have to witness in person.

Conversations with Richard continued. I was so comfortable with this man, which was unusual for me. A man of his status, a self-made millionaire, who attended fashion shows and traveled internationally, would normally have intimidated me. I would have felt like I wasn't good enough. That's the thing about on-line dating and being able to meet people outside of your normal circles. It is exciting! If we don't have the guts or nerve to get in our cars and drive, then people like the Magic Mirror Man may never cross our paths.

So, on this one day, I had an opportunity to jump in my camaro and drive to Nashville, Tennessee and meet the Magic Mirror Man!

We met in Franklin, Tennessee at Applebee's. I pulled into the parking lot and I was on the telephone with him. He caught a glimpse of the camaro before I had an opportunity to spot him. So he got out of his truck and walked over to my car. I got out of the car and "checked him out." He was taller than me, and he had on cowboy boots! He was truly an attractive man. We went into the restaurant and sat in the bar and ordered a margarita.

Sitting across the table from Richard was fun. His eyes lit up! He was definitely attracted to me, as I was to him. His voice. His accent. Yes, I was captured. We began to talk. Richard asked, "Have I told you about the time that I lived in Prattville, Alabama?" And he had not, so he proceeded. "Well, when I was a young man, I lived in your lovely (Roll Tide) state. I remember my first business. I came up with the idea of the roving billboard. I won't ever forget going into the bank and walking over to the lady loan officer. That one hundred foot walk seemed like a mile as I walked up to her and presented her with my business plan. She looked up at me and said *'did you write this yourself?'* I smiled as I told her that I did. That was my first business. My second business was creating placements for restaurants…you know the ones…with the advertisements on them."

I sat and took in all of his words, listening to each and every one as his accent reveled in my ears. "You are truly a self-made millionaire, aren't you?" I asked. He smiled. Humbled himself (although, I don't think he had to humble himself at all…I think he is just a humble man), and nodded his head. Yes.

"Tell me about your plan," he said. Wow, now I must say that I was impressed. This meant that he had truly read my profile. With excitement and passion about my plan, I began to explain, "I am writing a book." Before I could go into any more detail than that, Richard interjected, "Oh NO! I am research!"

"What?" I asked. "What are you talking about?" I was totally lost. I was talking about my accounting guidebook that I was planning to write, how in the world could he be research? "I am research for your book…your book. You are writing a book on your on-line dating experiences, aren't you?"

And there came my idea. "No, I am not! But, I can! I have some interesting stories to tell!"

We sat and talked for several hours, and I learned a lot about this man. I learned enough about him that I looked at him and said, "I want to go home with you tonight. I do. I like you and I am very attracted to you, but I know you well enough that if I go home with you, I will never hear from you again. You are a busy man. You won't have time for me." Richard knew that what I was saying was true. He commented, "You are very perceptive, Sandy. You have been doing this a while haven't you?" Then, he went on to say, "You will hear from me tomorrow. If you go home with me or if you don't go home with me, you will still hear from me tomorrow."

Was he telling me the truth? He is right. I have been doing this a while. And I have learned a lot about men. Men still like to be the hunters...the pursuers. Once they have you, they have met their goal, and they are gone. Something told me this man was different! He really didn't date much. Something told me that I could believe in him.

He walked me to the car. Standing by the car, he gave me the sweetest kiss, and then he said, "I have an idea, Sandy. Why don't you get in your car and follow me to my house in Nashville. I will take a shower and then you can give me a ride in that hot car of yours to Kentucky. That will give us a chance to talk and get to know each other."

This sounded intriguing. I loved the challenge of a road trip. I think he knew that already, and he put the challenge out there! "Okay," I said. "Let's do it! As long as you promise that you will call me tomorrow." His reassuring kiss said it all. Yes! I would go home with him and Yes, he would call me tomorrow. The Magic Mirror Man created magic in my heart!

I got in my car, keyed his address into my GPS (in case I lost him in traffic) and began to follow the Magic Mirror Man to his home in Nashville. The more I drove, the more I realized that I couldn't do this! I began to question myself. What are you doing, Sandy? You really don't know this man! He seems so different from anyone you have ever met. He is so transparent about who he is. He has been open and honest with you. He sat right there and told you that you were perceptive. You know you will never hear from this man again! I called Richard and said, "Please, say you won't be mad at me if I change my mind. I just can't go home with you. I don't feel right about it." Of course he would not be mad.

I could have turned around and drove back to North Alabama. I could have. But, I didn't. I drove toward downtown Nashville. Toward the home of my Familyman333 (you will meet him in a later chapter).

Over the course of the next several weeks, I still communicated with Richard. We stayed in contact for a while, believing in the connection that was made. I began to become entrepreneurial about the Magic Mirror and offered my marketing ideas. I called Richard one day and said, "I have an idea, Richard. The Magic Mirror. It is an incredible concept! Is it affordable to your every day middle-class household?" Not quite! Each mirror cost about $5,000.00. My thoughts: "Every woman feels fat...even if she is a size 2. Why not allow EVERY woman an opportunity to put on sexy lingerie for her man without ever having to take her clothes off! Yes women and men both would enjoy this one!"

"And let's take this thing mobile! What about pre-selecting thousands of formal dresses. Then take the Magic Mirror to schools several months before prom and allow each girl an opportunity to stand in front of the mirror and allow the magic to transform them into the beauty that they will be on prom night. With the push of a button, the dress could be ordered and sitting on their front porch the next day! Apply this same concept to wedding/bridal attire! Yes, Mr. Richard, we have to take this thing mobile! Hire me!"

As I presented my marketing ideas to the Magic Mirror Man, he explained that they had already thought of these same ideas. I was a little too late, but not a little too excited! I had enjoyed meeting this man and the exciting life that he lived. However, I never had an opportunity to see him again. His busy life took him away into another world, never to be seen again. I did make contact one last time with Richard to remind him about my book. I told him that because he gave me the idea about the book that he should be able to tell me how his story ends. So I ask him. "How should our story end? It should be magical." His response: "It's a never ending story!" I replied, "The magic of the Magic Mirror allows time to stand still, so that the gorgeous, sexy man can pursue his career and raise his children until Bamagirlluvsu becomes his renewed priority." Mmmmmmm. I like it... the never-ending story to the magic mirror. Maybe this should be the last chapter.....

NOT!

The Magic Mirror Man is a wonderful man and his priorities are what they are. I heard from him one last time... for him to say... "Sandy, you are a wonderful lady, and I like you, but I am just too busy to pursue a relationship. I wish you luck!"

I was blessed to meet the Magic Mirror Man. This is one of the people that came into my life for a reason. The reason(s): So, that I could learn that it doesn't matter the status people are in life, the rich...the poor...we are all still human and can connect with each other. Sandy is worthy. I also learned that money doesn't mean everything in this world! (I know, it helps)! I am sorry for the Magic Mirror Man that he may always be too busy to reach out and find real love. Maybe one day, his success will provide him the time to be happy in other areas of his life.

And...I was provided with the inspiration of this book! Bamagirlluvsu in PRINT!

As for the Magic Mirror, I will sit back and wait for it to become a reality, as I believe we will all be seeing this in our local malls soon. And I will reminisce about the time that I actually met the Magic Mirror Man.

If only we could use the Magic Mirror to create the perfect man – standing in front of the mirror, and with a swipe of a hand, we piece together our ideal soul mate, one piece at a time, a small part of each man that we ever met – the parts that we grew attached to and learned to love – Swipe! Poof! Swipe! Poof! The perfect man! If it were only that simple!

Song Application - "The Man in the Mirror" – Michael Jackson©

♥♥Invest In Me♥♥

Sometimes in the on-line dating world, I would meet someone. Life would happen, they would get lost in cyber-space, and then they would appear again. With so many opportunities available on the website, you can easily lose someone in the mix. How do we know when we chat with someone, then we get busy chatting with others, and we get busy with our "real" life, that we might miss out on our Mr. Right? We don't know. And, I guess we can be lucky enough, for that person to find us and make contact again.

That is what happened with me and Mr. "Invest In Me." We met briefly. Exchanged a few chats. Emailed for a while. Had a few telephone calls. During the process of getting to know each other, he mentioned the reason for his screen name. He was not an investor by profession, but instead dabbled a little by passion. It was a hobby that he enjoyed. My middle child had indicated he would love to invest in the stock market as a result of an economics project in high school. So there was a brief discussion with Mr. Investor about this.

Then...Life Happened. I met someone. I met "the Baby Daddy." At this time, I sent a text to all potential dates in my life informing them that I had met someone and I wanted to see where it went. So, Mr. Investor was kicked to the curb. My POF© profile was blocked so that I could pursue this new relationship with the Baby Daddy.

Months later, while online once again, when "the Baby Daddy" was busy being "the Baby Daddy," I unblocked my profile and began fishing again. There...out of the blue (sea)...came an email once again from Mr. Investor. "It must not have worked out with your home-town guy," he said. I replied, "No, it didn't." Of course, he questioned why, and I proceeded to explain what happened. We exchanged phone numbers again and began to try to recapture memories of previous conversations. He kept saying to me, "I know you will remember our conversations after a while." I laughed. Me! You have got to be kidding! Thinking to myself about how many potential dates I had chatted with since I talked with Mr. Investor months ago. There is no way I would recall ANY conversation we had. The conversations about stock investments came to mind only because of his screen name.

This was funny to me. Being as open as I am, I proceeded to explain to Mr. Investor that there was no way I would remember those conversations. It was really best that we put the past behind us and start anew! He agreed. And that is just what we did. We had several conversations, and then I revealed to him that I had a one-day training class in Memphis at the Peabody. I would be in Memphis the very next week. This would give us a chance to meet!

Was this luck? Or was it fate! Would this give me a chance to meet someone that I was meant to meet months before? My desire to seek the signs of the universe or for God to show me what I am supposed to do drove me to consider this a direct indication that I was meant to meet Mr. Investor. So we made plans to meet at the bar at the Peabody.

It was four days before that trip and the predetermined meeting would occur. Many conversations took place where we began to get to know each other a little better. A lot of stories were told (including me sharing many of my on-line dating stories) and him sharing stories about whom he was and where he had been. As I have said so many times. We all have a story to tell. We all have a past.

The day prior to my drive to Memphis, Mr. Investor sent me a text asking me this question: "All the choices below are obviously important, but I want to know which one (or two) is most important to you? In other words, what could I do on a daily basis that would always remind you that you picked the right guy and always felt loved? The choices are: gifts…acts of service…physical touch…quality time…or words of appreciation? No rush at all, but I do want to get a sneak peek behind that beautiful smile and see what makes you feel good or special in a relationship?"

Wow, what a question? This man was really interested in me. He was really making an effort to get to know me. Now, I must disclose about the danger cell phones and texting can have because the message didn't come through as beautifully as I have written it above. It took quite a few texts and a telephone conversation to actually get to the root of what was being asked. The message was scrambled because the part of the texts with the list of choices was missing. Somehow it did not send along with the other texts. You know how LONGGGGG texts can be sometimes. The message won't completely send, or some of it gets sent later and the messages can come through scrambled – out of order. Well, that is what happened with this message. Not getting the list, I replied to the text, "Are you going to send me my choices?" He answered, "They are in the texts, silly. Then you leave the details up to me. Rotflmbo" (if you don't know texting acronyms, look it up – LOL).

Funny. I never received the list. So, I called him. He gave me my choices. And I began to explain to him why I felt the way that I did. "They are all important," I said. "But allow me to share a story." When I was married previously, my husband asked me what I wanted for Christmas. My reply was, "There isn't anything material that you could give me that would be what I would want. I would love to have a weekend away with you. You see. We recently had a child, and therefore had very little intimate, alone time together. Alone time would have meant so much more than receiving anything material. My ex did not listen. He instead bought me a diamond ring. It hurt my feelings that he didn't take the time to listen to my wants and needs." I explained all of this to Mr.

Investor as I gave him my defiant answer. "I would rather have quality time with you any day, with words of appreciation having a very close second. I like knowing I am appreciated and needed."

Fair enough. Wow. He appreciated my answer and began to tell me how much my story revealed about myself to him. He admired and respected my answer. And I asked, "What about you?" He expected that question. After all, I should want to know that about him as well. His reply was, "physical touch and words of appreciation. I also, like to be appreciated," he said. Of course he liked physical touch. What man doesn't! No. I shouldn't say that. I shouldn't think that! What female doesn't like physical touch? What human doesn't like physical touch? WE ALL WANT AND NEED THAT! There are just other things that go along with that touch that provides us all with that unique intimate experience.

That evening, before going to bed, we talked and sent our final nightly texts. I explained to him that I felt like a kid at Christmas, anticipating Christmas Day and the joy that goes along with it. Meeting someone new always brings a little joy and a little anticipation. And I was soooooo anticipating meeting this new man. He sounded so incredible on the phone. And during our many conversations that week, he showed such an interest in what was going on in my life and in my children's lives. He had three sons himself, so he understood the time that it takes to raise children. This could be it for me! This could be the one! (AGAIN!) Yes, anticipation was a definite emotion that was in my heart and mind.

The next morning, when I awoke, I sent Mr. Investor a text. "Merry Christmas!" I said. He replied, "Christmas huh?" "Yes sir," I said. "Are we exchanging presents?" he asked. My response had to be clever. I thought about our conversation from the day before and replied the only response that would fit...the appropriate and only answer was "There isn't anything material that you could give me that would be what I want…LOL." Yes. That was the perfect response. His response was just as clever, "I know! I listened last night. LOL. If we hit it off, I will trade you a little quality time for a kiss and holding hands!" Awwwwww. A sweet trade-off. My first choice from the list exchanged with his first choice on the list. It's a win-win!

I probably should not have shared my book-writing venture with Mr. Investor, but for some reason I felt the desire to share my entrepreneurial side with him. So I began to express this side of me to him by saying, "I must preface this story by expressing to you that you are not research. But, I am writing a book about my on-line dating experiences. Don't worry. I already have sufficient material for the book, I don't need any more. I don't want you worrying all evening that I am taking notes for the book." With hesitation, he replied, "Uuuuhhhhhh, really. Well, you never know what could happen that might be book-worthy. Things tend to happen when I'm around." He laughed.

I could not wait to get on the road! I already knew exactly what I would do. I was going to arrive at the hotel early. Check in. Arrive at my room. Lie down on the bed for a while for a rest. To achieve a new invigorated feeling, so that I would be more alert and not appear tired. Take a quick bath. Freshen up. Be recharged and ready to meet my new potential partner.

The drive to Memphis was a great one filled with mixed emotions and that sweet anticipation of meeting my new man. He seemed so into me. I hope he likes me. I hope I like him. There had been so many previous dates in which either myself or the date would immediately recognize that the attraction or chemistry just wasn't there. No-one is to blame. That's life. The hardest part is when YOU think everything went well, but the other person returns with, "I just don't see this working!"

So, yes, I made that drive to Memphis, keeping in mind that the possibility would exist that this may be just another "fish in the sea!"

When I was about an hour from Memphis, I sent him a text, "I am getting a little nervous now," I said. His reply, "It's just the traffic. LOL. Once you get to the room, I am sure you will feel better." I recall thinking, how sweet that was for him to reassure me. He didn't want me to feel nervous. He was trying to alleviate my concerns. Yes. I think I like this guy.

I finally arrived at the hotel, checked in, and took the elevator to my room. When I walked into my room, I could not believe my eyes! Wow! Yes. Wow! There were roses all over the room. (My first thoughts: "Oh no. Familyman333 did this – read about him in the next chapter. I felt guilty, like I was cheating on him, but I knew I wasn't). Someone had really put a lot of forethought and effort into how these roses would be placed. There were three lying straight ahead on the king-sized bed, one on the night stand, and three more lying at the foot of the bed with a card. A really sweet card that read… "I wanna spend quality time with you." (That is when I knew it wasn't Familyman333).

Walking into the restroom, there were three more roses in the corner of the vanity, leaning against the mirror, one lying across the white towels, and one leaning in the corner of the shower. It was absolutely beautiful! My heart fell. I couldn't breathe for a moment. I picked up the phone and called Mr. Investor.

"You didn't!" I exclaimed. "Wow! This is beautiful! I am going to take pictures!" He replied, "I knew you had a pretty tough day today and yesterday, and I thought you deserved something nice!" Again. This was unbelievable! Then, I had to ask, "So, did you tell them how to strategically place these roses in the room?" His answer as he laughed a little mischievous laugh, "Honestly, I did it myself. They let me into the room. I had a lot of fun!"

I had never had anyone do this before! This was unbelievable. Sweet! He really thought about me. And the card… "I wanna spend quality time with you!" He listened. A man really listened to what I said. He acknowledged my needs…my desires. Yes, this could really be the man for me! "Where are you?" I inquired. "I am downstairs in the lobby," He said. "Allow me to freshen up and I will be right down," I said.

I quickly freshened up. My plan of relaxing and taking my time to prepare for this meeting was completely blown away. Blown away! But, that was okay. I had a new adrenaline rush going on in my body! I suddenly wasn't tired anymore! I couldn't have rested anyway! I hurriedly changed my clothes, freshened up, and headed down to the lobby. I could not wait!

When I got to the lobby, I called him. I saw the man walking just ahead of me take his phone to his ear. "Where are you?" I asked. "I am in the lobby…" he said. Then he turned around and our eyes met. We took a seat in the lobby and began to talk and laugh. This was an incredible meeting. He looked much better than his on-line pictures. That is very unusual, especially with my prior experiences with false advertisers. This man was beautiful! I could tell by his first look at me that the feeling was mutual. His thoughts. His feelings. Everything was revealed through the glimmer in his eyes. He reached out and grasped my hand. And we kissed. A sweet, slow, gentle kiss. Yes. The kiss was sensual. We had gotten past the kiss. Whew! The evening was definitely off to a good start!

We proceeded to the bar. As we sat across from each other, our eyes met. We could not stop smiling. We both had that "shit-eatin" grin on our faces. Yes. That is what we call it here in the South. That grin that you get on your face that looks like you have been up to something…you know the one…like you just got yourself into some shit that you can't get out of. And the look on your face lets everyone around you know that you are guilty! We both had that look. And we could not stop smiling. "Wow!" He said. "Wow!" Again and Again. Over and over. His interrogatory "Wow" kept projecting from his sensuous mouth. I felt like I was the perfect Christmas gift that really wowed my receiver! No-one could ask for a better compliment!

Mr. Investor had indicated in previous conversations that it had been a very long time since he had drank a margarita. He would never drink and drive. It was five o'clock. So, I insisted that he drink a margarita with me. "It's okay," I said. "One margarita won't hurt you. It is only five o'clock. We can always walk around a while. You have many hours to alleviate any feelings of intoxication." So, he agreed. We ordered an appetizer and sat and enjoyed the conversation. As the bottom of the glass began to appear, the waitress made her way toward our table. "Can I get you another one?" she inquired. "Yes, I said. WE will BOTH have one more!" I looked at him and smiled. "It's okay," I said. There is a sofa in the room. You can sleep on the sofa!" He smiled. I followed jokingly with, "You knew the roses were your insurance policy, didn't you?" We both laughed. Yes. This was a good night.

We walked back to the room, hand in hand. We both knew everything had gone well. The attraction was definitely there. It was a sweet meeting. Once in the room, we prepared the sofa for his nights rest. We sat and talked for what seemed like hours. We began to kiss. His kisses were great. Sensual. The way he would extend his tongue from his mouth and allow me to maneuver my lips and tongue around his, turned us both on. It was a variation of the kiss that I had never experienced before. And he possessed the perfect tongue for that purpose. Wow! Yes. Again. Wow! We both knew that tonight wasn't the night to pursue anything sexual, but it was the night for EVERYTHING sensual. Touching. Kissing. Caressing. Then falling asleep in each others' arms. We both got what we wanted for Christmas that night. Quality Time and Physical Touch. I must add that I believed I received all five of the items in the list that night. Everything he did. Everything he said. All were at the top of my list.

Morning arrived. The time had come that we must part ways. I was in town for training, so I had to head downstairs to the conference room. Mr. Investor left the hotel room, but not without leaving me with one of those sensual kisses to remember him by, sending blood-rushing waves throughout the rest of my body. Yes, there would definitely be more quality time shared between us in the future.

I left Memphis that evening with as much excitement in which I had arrived. But that excitement was also accompanied by a little sadness. Sadness that I was traveling away from Memphis back to North Alabama. Life would continue to happen. Children and work responsibilities awaited at home. Planning ahead for more of that quality time and those sensual kisses would definitely have to be a part of my future.

Invest in YOU

"I am going to send you a text," he said. "Read it. Then await my telephone call. I want to share something with you." I received the text. And yes, it made absolutely no sense whatsoever. I awaited the telephone call. As I sat in my bed, laptop in hand, Mr. Investor proceeded to tell me about a speculative investment opportunity in which I had a chance to recover with phenomenal returns. Yes, this was big! And yes, he believed in it. He had heard my stories of struggle (kids, job). He knew something and he thought he should allow me to be a part of it.

I am not going to reveal this investment strategy in my book. Not because I don't want to share in the wealth, but because, if this thing turns out to be a complete flop, I don't want to be embarrassed about my eagerness to listen and take advice from a man that I hardly knew. By the time this book is released, maybe I will know more and can share. In the meantime, know that I Googled.© I read. I researched. I made my own decision based on economics and some insight that I also had. If I make it big with this, we will all know that the decision paid off. My meeting of Mr. "Invest in Me," allowed me to invest quality time in a man that took the time to invest in me… this would truly be the investment that had a return that was tenfold…it would be the investment that keeps on giving!

Home Sweet Home

Not much time had passed. It had been less than forty-eight hours since I left Mr. Investor in Memphis, Tennessee. I felt a closeness to this man. I wanted to see him again. He had shared an investment strategy with me and he didn't even know me. This man cared about me and my well-being. I sent him a text, "I want to see you again." I said. "I like you." His reply, "I think that is a great idea!" I proceeded with my next text…the question… "Where in Memphis do you live?"

A telephone call followed. "Sandy," he began quietly and timidly, "I wanted to answer your question with simple directions, but felt my response required more information, so I thought I should call you. So here is the story. I have a nice home, and it is currently rented out. I then moved into an apartment…" As he began his story, I was thinking, oh no. He is ashamed of where he lives. Apartments aren't so bad. I wish I lived in an apartment right now. No upkeep. Cheaper….. Okay….he continued with his statement. "I then moved all of my things to storage and I am sleeping in my car now."

"What?" I questioned. "Really?" "No way. You are kidding!" He wasn't kidding. He continued explaining to me that he had lost his job, was doing a little contracting work on the side, but things had gotten tough due to the ex-wife and children in college, etc. Wow! I didn't know quite what to say. He was so uplifted! He wasn't feeling sorry for himself! He was actually laughing at himself. For a brief moment, I shed a few tears. Tears of empathy. I could not imagine what he was going through. Every possible vision went through my head. My eyes began to tear as I recalled that Mr. Investor had no siblings and his Mom and Dad had both passed. His three boys were away at college on loans, grants and scholarships, so they were taken care of, but he had no-one.

For a few moments, I empathized. I wanted to offer him a place to stay. I am always the one trying to help others, wanting to make everything okay. But this would not be a good idea. I have a daughter at home, so I relinquished the thought.

Even though this was no comparison to where this man was at this time in his life, I was reminded of the time in my life when I was poor. My mother was sick, first with rheumatoid arthritis and then cancer. I was fourteen. I had to go to work and support the family or we didn't eat. We were living in a small frame house below a bridge. I think probably we were living there on Section 8 subsidy, even though my Mom wouldn't ever tell me that. I was working 48 hours a week so that my Mom, myself and my two siblings could live. I didn't question why I had to do this. I just did it. I didn't have the opportunity to live the typical "teenage" life. (Maybe that's why I am so young now – LOL).

My memory turned back to that house we lived in. It was roach infested due to the flooding of the creek nearby, and the water flowed into the house on multiple occasions. As I recalled the times, my siblings and I would carry chairs into the kitchen, turn out all the lights, to provide darkness and security to the little roaches, and then flip the switch. We would stand in those chairs, with fly swats in hand and play a game of "who could kill the most bugs."

Recalling this time of entertainment, I had a grin on my face. And so I couldn't help but laugh with Mr. Investor. Not at him! But, with him! He was definitely not down on himself at all. He reminded me a lot of myself. Then his question brought me back to his reality, "What are you thinking?" he asked.

Well, being the brutally, honest person that I am, I said, "It's going in the book! I am sorry, but this has to go in the book!" We both laughed. "This is really good," I continued. "You must look at this from my perspective. I met you. I am thinking by your screen name that you may have even made a few great investments. I took advice from you on investing and you are living in your car! I took investment advice from a homeless man!"

And I continued without taking a breath, "You brought me roses. As an insurance policy. This is priceless. An insurance policy that you would have a place to sleep that night. OMG, where did you get the roses? Did you pick them from someone's garden? See, this is good! Oh, and the couch. I made you sleep on the couch! While I slept in that great big comfy king-size bed! I am so sorry! I ordered two margaritas for both of us...what if you hadn't had the money to pay for them? What if I had ordered a really big meal? See, this gets better and better!

OMG. Last night, I kept telling you that it was okay for you to leave whenever you wanted. I said that over and over. That if you felt there was no connection with me and you wanted to leave, that you could leave. Wow! I could have been the ugliest girl in the world, and you would have stayed...just to have a place to sleep. Yes, it has to go in the book. I know that I told you that you weren't research, but this has to go in the book!" Whew!

We all know that we interact with others daily. Watching them smile. Listening to their laughter, as many put on a pretense to cover up what is really going on in their lives. This is a true example of not knowing what really goes on at home....

Mr. Investor is a kind man. Caring. I wanted to offer him a place to stay, but knew that I couldn't do that. But that is who I am. At the writing of this book, I am still waiting on the investment to pay off, and who knows, maybe Mr. Investor will turn into the investment that keeps on giving. He surely made me laugh....and cry....as I made the daily phone call to him to ask, "Are you home yet?"

As you read into the next chapter, you will discover why I never saw Mr. Investor again. Despite the fact that he seemed to have a jealous nature, believing that it was difficult for a male and female to have a friendship. This made me fear that he would never be able to handle my out-going personality. It was best that we part ways. And so I moved on...again.

♥♥Family Man (333)♥♥

1111. There it is again. The number 1111. I have seen this number over and over for about four years now. In the beginning, it was rare. I would see the number and think to myself. "1111"….mmmmmm….. A fleeting thought. And it was gone. As time went on, the number 1111 began to appear more frequently. On the clock beside my bed, on my cell phone, the television, telephone numbers on the side of cars or trucks, billboards. The number 1111 was everywhere!

About two years ago, I was home cleaning house. We all hate that chore and will look for any excuse to break away from it, won't we? So, as I am cleaning house, I see the time. It is 11:11. Mmmmmm. There it is again. I continue cleaning. Another fleeting thought. I decided to turn the television on a music channel. So, I do. Across the screen, there it is again "11 am til 11 pm." 1111 once again. Being a numbers fanatic, I decided to Google©. "What is the significance of the number 1111?"

Page after page of items returned in my search about the "1111 Phenomenon." Wow! What is this? There are a lot of people besides me seeing these numbers! Incredible! So, I randomly selected an entry and began to read: "In the beginning God sent one thousand, one hundred eleven (1,111) angels to earth to protect his people."

Ok. Ok. I must stop right here and I preface this entire story with the words, I AM SKEPTICAL! I AM! I am skeptical, but I also will never be a person that will say it can never happen. I will also say that I know anyone can put ANYTHING on the internet. So, I proceeded with my reading and with my skepticism…

"If you are seeing the number 1111, then it means that angels are trying to contact you. They need you to do something for them. Because God gives us the right to free will, we can say – "Tell me what you want me to do" ...OR... "Leave me alone, I am not interested." Wow, I think. Angels contacting me? Yeah, sure! Skepticism. Skepticism. But, I continued with my reading. The article began to describe some of the various angels by number and what they represented. This is when my skepticism began to lighten, and cold chills appeared on my arms. "Angel number 333 was sent to protect the sick."

Angel 333. Could it be? Is it possible? Several years earlier, my twin brother's wife was diagnosed with lung cancer. Before she passed away, she had a stroke. She could not speak. Not one word. Nothing. No communication. Except....when she would point into the air and repeatedly say "3-3-3...3-3-3" over and over. Followed by the words "talking to." That was it. Over and over. "333, 333...talking to talking to."

I must say the memory of her, before she died, knowing that she was leaving my brother with a mentally challenged daughter to raise alone was overwhelming. Could it be that she was seeing an angel? Could it be that God sent an angel to Susan, so that she could part this world knowing that her daughter would be okay? Wow. Angel #333 was with Susan during that time. God sent Angel #333 to protect the sick.

So, I read the article about the number 1111 and the number 333. I have shared this story with many people during the last several years. These two sets of numbers appear to me more frequently as time goes by. At one time, I was driving Interstate 75 to Gainesville, Georgia to see my sister. This was in April, 2011 right after the tornadoes devastated the South. I looked at my clock. Of course, it was 11:11. I looked up and noted that I was at exit 333. Okay, this was the first time that I had ever seen both numbers simultaneously. I raised my hands in the air (yes I was driving, so it was only briefly....but I was okay….after all….angels were with me) and I said out loud: "Alright, already! Tell me what you want me to do!" I would love to tell you that an angel appeared and told me what to do. Or that I received some sign from above, but absolutely nothing happened. Absolutely nothing.

Did this stop me from looking for the numbers 1111 and 333? No. Did the numbers continue to appear to me? Of course. After all, the numbers were a part of me now. I had connected the "333" angel with my deceased sister-in-law and my skepticism was not so much anymore. And after all…. "It could happen"….. "Angels in the Outfield©" (Movie application this time….smiling).

I don't need to tell you that when I received an email from Familyman333, that it caught my attention. Of course it did. After all, the "333" was my captive number. And his profile said it all.

He loved the water. As I said, most all people online love the beach or the lake. And Familyman333 was no exception. Then, the fact that he was a hopeless romantic, and enjoyed doing all of the old-fashioned things really captured my attention. After all, didn't I change my profile at one point so that I would attract this kind of man? I wanted someone old-fashioned, who believed in the courtship and treating his lady with mutual respect and honor. So, when I received his email, it really caught my attention. His email was sweet. A kind man, I thought. He loved my profile. And I responded. I had to respond. I must. I really had no choice, did I? So, I replied.

Familyman333 and I had many emails and chats. Then we exchanged phone numbers. He was the most attentive man. He recognized me for someone that he was attracted to and he wanted to get to know me. The more we talked, the more we realized that there was definitely a connection.

We became new Facebook© friends. I began to take a stroll through his profile. You can tell a lot about a person by looking at their Facebook© profile. I could see that he had a good "family" life. There were many pictures of himself with his children. Everyone always looked so happy. I became a little envious, wishing my children and I had this relationship. My children were younger, with much maturing to be done. His children were in their late 20's and early 30's. They had surpassed the era of Mom and Dad being stupid, and reached the period of time in which Mom and Dad are smarter than they gave them credit.

Familyman333 was an older gentleman. I think that is why he was such an attraction in the beginning. The older man really knows how to treat a woman. He grew up in the era that respect was not only inherent, it was granted. No questions asked. That is just the way he was supposed to be. It wasn't his choice. It was just his character.

Continuing to look at his Facebook© to learn more about this new intriguing, captivating man, suddenly I stopped. Breathless. Speechless. Taken aback. There it was! AGAIN! Those numbers. Not 333. But the number 1111. Could it be? Familyman333's birthday is November 11. 11 11. Wow! Is it possible that the angels were guiding me to this man?

Years earlier, when I found the website that conveyed the meanings of these numbers and found that seeing the number "1111" meant that the angels wanted me to do something, I assumed that meant to do something to help someone else. Of course, I would assume that. That is what I do! That is who I am! But is it possible that the angels really didn't want me to do anything at all? Is it possible that the real objective behind my seeing these numbers all of these years was so that I would be drawn to this man when we crossed paths? Wow! Now, you know that there is no question at all. I HAD TO MEET THIS MAN!

As I ventured through his photos, I again was captivated! Among the pictures of Familyman333 and his family, was a picture of him and Lee Ann Womack! Again! I was captured! It was as if a magnet was drawing me in. What could I do? I could not escape this man and I did not want to. I was drawn to him and I must meet him! I had to call Familyman333. I had to tell him my story. Our story.

"Bruce," I said. (Yes, I shall call him Bruce, because my son stated that he looked like Bruce Willis – LOL) "I have to share something with you. I have to meet you! I must! You see, we are meant to meet. I just know it!" As I reiterated the story behind the numbers "333" and "1111" and that his screen name and birthday were representative of both, he got caught up in the idea of the angels just as much as I was. He appreciated my outlook and the excitement that was exemplary of my voice and laughter. Although I wasn't a religious person, I still believed. This story was a remarkable imagery of my faith. This newly discovered detail about my personality drew Bruce in a little closer. He now knew that he had to meet me too!

We arranged to meet one Saturday evening. It was a last minute plan. No pre-planning for us. Spontaneity is the spice of life. And after all, doesn't Bamagirlluvsu gravitate to the adventure of a road trip? Of course she does. So, plans were made and it was decided. Bamagirlluvsu would meet Familyman333 tonight.

I jumped in my red camaro and headed toward Nashville. And he jumped in his F-150 pickup and headed toward Huntsville. Bamagirlluvsu driving I-65 North and Familyman333 driving I-65 South. Let's make this a little more exciting. We had absolutely no idea where we were going to meet. None at all. So, we added a little more intrigue, and a little fear, to the trip. We decided that we would both drive. And drive. Until we met. We were on the telephone, so we could both dictate to the other one where we were at all times. When we got close to the same mile marker on Interstate-65, that would become our meeting spot.

"What am I doing?" I thought. "Am I crazy?" I am driving to meet a man that I don't know (not like this was the first time I had done this) and I am driving to nowhere....Where? I couldn't send myself the traditional email about where I was going because I didn't even know where I was going. Yes, I was definitely stepping outside my comfort zone. But, something made it all okay. It was the numbers. I truly believed that the angels were with me. I somehow just knew that I was going to be safe. I was okay.

Finally, we crept closer and closer to each other. We were there, but just where "there" was I didn't know. Lewisburg, Tennessee, Exit 22. As I turned into the exit lane, I began searching the signs for available places to meet...a nice restaurant...a bar...something! There was absolutely nothing! A McDonalds, a Subway, and a truck stop. I pulled into the truck stop and called Familyman333 to tell him about our choices. Our "romantic" road trip ended with the two of us parking in front of the "shower" entrance for truck drivers.

When the two of us got out of our vehicles and walked toward each other, we were both laughing so hard that we could barely speak. We knew this was a funny story...our story...of the first time we would meet. Who would ever believe this? How could we ever forget the night that we first met? At a truck stop, at Exit 22 (which, by the way is 11+11), at 9:00 at night, in the middle of nowhere. We sat on the tailgate and talked briefly. We were there just long enough to meet and see if there was an initial attraction. He kissed me on the cheek and I got in my red camaro for the drive back home.

That is all it takes to know, right? A brief meeting? All anyone needs is a little time to see if there is chemistry between the two of you. I think you know immediately! It is there or it isn't. That was my thoughts with Engineer4 earlier that year. Right?

I was a little distraught as I made my way back to North Alabama. This was supposed to be right! This man was supposed to be it…the man of my dreams! He was supposed to be my angel, sent by God.   All of the signs were there, 1111 and 333. And OMG, Lee Ann Womack. She is supposed to sing at my funeral! (Forget that CD I have on my bedside table for each of my kids…I can now have the real thing). Something is all wrong. Just wrong! I followed my heart…Why couldn't this be my happily ever after?

A few minutes after being on the road, I received a text from Bruce. "Thank you for meeting me. I could tell you weren't interested, but you handled it with grace and style. I am hoping that we can be friends."   My eyes revealed it all. He knew. He knew that something wasn't right. I didn't really have to say anything…he just knew.   It showed in my eyes.

Of all the men that I have met, this one was the one that showed a real heart. He was genuine. He was a simple man…kind…caring…with honor and pride. This man touched me somehow. I wasn't sure why or how? But, there was something about him. My mind told me, "Sandy, he is old…too old for you...move forward and don't look back. This is over. You can walk away. You have done this so many times before. Just walk."

I couldn't walk. I drove away. But, I could not walk away. I didn't realize what was happening. I subconsciously remained in his life. The telephone. Texting. Chatting. It didn't stop. "We can be friends," I said, "Lifelong friends." The more we talked. The more I wanted to see him again. My heart began to get involved as I listened to his conversations about his four children and his employees. As I heard how he helped an employee whose family was sick in another state and Bruce gave him money to get home. As I listened to him tell about a young man, needing work, but he had a past and Bruce didn't know whether to give him a chance or not…so he asked him to work with him a few days so that he could get to know his heart. He wanted to gain a comfort level with him. Then he introduced him to a friend who later hired him and the young man will forever be grateful.

The conversations were funny at times. Then serious. Then funny again. Through these conversations I discovered some things about Bruce. His genuine honor and respect in his personal life had led him to a place in his career where he decided to open his own business, a dry-cleaning business. "Bruce Willis Dry-Cleaning."

My thoughts from the name of the business, "This is a little mom and pop business, nothing more." Through further conversations, I found out that my "Family Man" had happened upon a real opportunity in Nashville, Tennessee. What is Nashville known for? Country music, of course. And who lives in Nashville? The singers…the stars.

Through hard work and dedication and by putting his heart into his business, Bruce happened upon a niche in Nashville. He became the man the stars (and other upper-class business people) could trust, not only with their personal belongings, but also with their lives. Not literally, but figuratively, these higher class people began to utilize the services of his dry-cleaning company as a masquerade for who they were. He became the man that would be called to deliver their dry-cleaning or even their new purchases to them. His ability to remain discreet earned him the trust of the Nashville community.

And yes. He knew Lee Ann Womack. He called me one day while standing in her home. I became so excited.

"Bruce!" I exclaimed like a child demanding attention. "Tell her. Tell her my story, please! Tell her about the books on my night stand with the CD's. That this is the song that I want played at my funeral. Tell her…OMG…Bruce, do you think she would sing the I Hope You Dance Song© at my funeral? I mean…I wouldn't know it if she did…but everyone there would know. Wow! I will take a picture of my books. Show it to her! Tell her my story!"

Bruce laughed at me. I was serious, but he laughed. I guess I was quiet amusing. The people he ran across daily had become an everyday occurrence with him. But to us out in the real world, this was huge. This was exciting! But Bruce was a humble man and not necessarily humbled by life's circumstances. I believe he was born that way. It was the heart and character that he had developed through precedential ethics and morals handed down from his parents.

We talked daily, every morning, during my morning commute and each evening during my evening commute, along with texts of genuine interest throughout the day. We were getting to know each other more and more. The more I talked with Familyman333, the more he captured my heart. I was beginning to feel a real connection to him. So, when he asked to drive to Huntsville and meet me for dinner, we both knew the answer would be yes!

The Courtship

Familyman333 was more than happy to make the two hour drive from Nashville to Huntsville to meet me for dinner. I picked the place. Chili's. I thought. It was on University Drive and easily located. We agreed to meet at 6:00 pm. When I arrived, he was already seated at a booth in the bar. I walked in and his eyes lit up. It was the same glimmer in the eyes that I had seen that evening at exit 22. Mr. Willis revealed everything in his eyes.

We each ordered a margarita and an appetizer as we sat and talked. We already felt that we knew each other, so conversation was easy. About an hour into the evening, I got up and moved to the other side of the table. I sat next to this man as I listened to his story about his marriage. He had been married for 20 years to a woman that didn't return his affection. So any act of attention, any reaction to his attention, gave him feelings of comfort and acceptance that he hadn't felt before.

My moving to his side of the table, and "flirting" with my eyes, as well as the subtle touch of my hand to his hand made his heart melt. I then crossed my legs toward him, as my dress fell just above my knee, providing an enticing view of the tan skin beneath, sending chills throughout his body. Wow, this was a feeling he hadn't experienced in a long time!

Then he began to tell me the sweet story about deciding what to wear. He called his daughter and asked for her expert "female" advice. "Wear a blue shirt, Dad. It will bring out the blue in your eyes." Bruce told this story with such humbleness. He wasn't embarrassed at all as he continued to tell the story. "I looked in my closet and there was no blue shirt. I told my daughter and she said, 'Well Dad, take a picture of the shirts in your closet and send it to me and I will tell you which one to wear!'" Priceless! I thought.

I looked at him, and I said, "You haven't been out on a date in a while, have you?" Bruce began to explain that he had devoted himself to his business and to his children. He had not really dated but he wanted to make an impression on me! I laughed with him as I told him that he looked very nice and I thought it was amazing that he had this relationship with his daughter.

I made my way outside, as he went to the restroom, and sat on a bench and waited. I was nervous and scared of what lie ahead, but there was something about this man. An innocence. A sweetness in his eyes. A gentleness in his touch. The way he valued his family like none other. The thrill of his profession as he had an association with various stars and important people in Nashville. There was an overwhelming desire for me to make Familyman333… well… uh… happy.

He joined me on the bench outside of Chili's and we continued to talk and flirt. With having had a little alcohol in our system, Bruce pointed across the street and said, "Guess what? There is a hotel across the street. Let's go over and I will get you a room for the night. I don't want you to drive home after having a few drinks." I anticipated that we might be drinking and not need to drive, so I packed a bag for the evening. "What about you?" I asked. This is when Mr. Willis revealed to me my first rule. "Remember the rule," he said. "Whatever Sandy wants."

Really. A rule. It has never been about what I want. I am the person that always takes care of everyone else. I am the person that makes sure everyone else is happy. Have I truly met someone that is going to think about me first? My needs will come first! "Whatever Sandy Wants." I like this rule!

As much as we both wanted for Mr. Willis to spend the night, we both knew that this was too soon. Bruce, having grown up in the "era" of the old-fashioned courtship, knew that he must return to Nashville. We both knew that our time together that evening was all it should have been. There would be future dates. A courtship, just like the one mentioned in my profile.

As I enjoyed my old-fashioned courtship, the day would arrive when the relationship would evolve into something more. Mr. Willis and I made arrangements to meet for dinner again. He drove to Huntsville to meet once more…in celebration of the place we had our first date.

This time was different. This time, we had more of an emotional attachment. After weeks of telephone calls, texting, and talking, we felt that we had grown in our relationship. So this time, when Mr. Willis suggested the hotel across the street…This time "Whatever Sandy Wants" would take on an entirely new meaning.

We drove across the street, stopping by the liquor store to purchase Bailey's Cream and Butterscotch schnapps. We were going to have buttery nipples. We had discovered through telephone calls that we both loved this drink, so we would share one (or two) in the room.

The nervousness and anticipation felt by both of us was evident. He didn't know exactly what was expected of him and neither did I. As the evening unfolded, we broke the ice by mixing the buttery nipples and toasting each other. We sat on the bed, drinking our delicious concoction and talking… touching… kissing. Mr. Willis and I were happy to be present in that room that night.

I excused myself briefly and went to the restroom to "get more comfortable." As I made my reappearance into the room, Bruce was standing at the vanity, mixing another drink. He turned and looked at me. There was the glimmer in the eyes again. He immediately stopped what he was doing, gently grabbed me, and pushed me against the wall. Then…there it was…THE KISS! You know the one. The one I had been waiting on all of my life. The one which that gentle force was just enough to represent the passion flowing in his body. He wanted me…and it showed in his kiss.

We made our way to the bed. He portrayed such innocence…such purity and inexperience. It had been such a long time since he had felt a woman. He wanted me, and that was obvious. But I felt a little guilty about being with this man. It was truly about him wanting and needing me. And yes, I wanted and needed him as well, but I was a little selfish. I needed to be needed! And this man really NEEDED me! Like no-one had ever needed me!

Crawling in bed with this man was easy. There was no hidden agenda. This man had a heart and it was revealed in all that he did. He kissed me gently. He caressed my body with a softness that I had never felt before "Slow down, Mr. Willis." I said. "We have the rest of our lives to enjoy each other." (Embellishment…Embellishment…Embellishment… OR NOT! You Decide)!

Familyman333's responses to my touch were incredible! And the way my body responded to his was just as unbelievable. The touching and caressing and kissing lasted for hours. As we collapsed into the sheets and closed our eyes to rest, our bodies gave way to a sense of belonging. We had a glimpse of the desire that our bodies had for each other. And, just for tonight, that was more than enough. What a night!

Song Application - "Just a Kiss" – Lady Antebellum©

Wishy-Washy

Phone calls and texts were numerous. That night was incredible, but came to an end. Bruce returned to Nashville and I returned to North Alabama. His affections and care were shown by his acts of kindness. He began by sending flowers. Beautiful flowers with a sweet card inscribed, "To the sweetest rose in Alabama." My heart revealed to me an attraction…a desire to see Bruce again. But my mind felt differently. My mind kept telling me, "Sandy, he is too old for you. I mean, you know he is only ten years older. He is 59. You are 49. It really isn't that different."

I read in a book one time that a person stops aging emotionally at the age that their parents die. In that case, I would be in my early 20's. And that is how I felt. Don't get me wrong. Logically, I knew better. I knew that I was 49! But, I didn't feel 49. And everyone told me that I didn't look 49. Of course, we want to believe what others say, especially when it is a compliment that we want to hear.

Why would I allow ten years to seem like such a huge difference? Why would this bother me so badly? After all, I have always known that my era...my missed era of life was that of the "Walton's" on "Walton's Mountain." I missed my era in life. Don't misunderstand. I am not Miss Susie Homemaker or anything at all like that. That is not the part of the era that I missed. The part that I missed was the peacefulness and the contentfulness of the lifestyle present during that period. That is the era that I belonged and Mr. Willis was from that era. "He's old-school," my son would later say. And "old school" isn't so bad, huh? "Old school" brought with it the inherent honor and respect of a man toward his woman. "Old school" was a good thing to be!

I began to share some of Bruce's stories with my children. I recall one specific story about a well-known music client. I won't convey that story or the client here. Confidences and discretion must be maintained. Upon telling the story to my son Jonathan, he said, "Mom, do you think Bruce can get his client to sign my fraternity book? He was in Sigma Chi fraternity!" I sent Bruce a text inquiring. He said, "Sandy, if you will make sure he was in Sigma Chi, I will ask him to sign the book."

I went to my woman cave, laptop in hand, and began to Google©, "the client and fraternities." About this time, I was on the telephone with Bruce and Izzy walked into the room. "What are you Googling©?" she asked. I explained to Izzy what was happening and she exclaimed, "Forget the fraternity! That man is sexy! I just want his autograph!"

Bruce, overhearing the comment said, "Tell Ms. Izzy that I will do her one better. Tell her to jump in that camaro with her Mom and make a road trip to Nashville and I will take her to my client's house and we will knock on the door and she can meet this man of her dreams!" Izzy was so excited. (BTW, we did take a road trip to Nashville later, and we did drive to the house and Izzy got to meet the man of her dreams). It was this type of story or deed that made life with Familyman333 never dull!

The argument between my heart and my mind continued. I told Bruce my concerns. I was honest with him and I could hear the disappointment in his voice. He knew that I was "too good to be true." He said that he knew that he would never have me for life, but he wanted me as long as he could have me. I was truly a joy to him. He had experienced things with me that he had never felt before!

I could not continue to see Bruce. It did not matter how he made me feel. This wasn't right. It just wasn't right. I kept going on-line searching for someone else to meet. And I told Bruce this as well. I wanted him to know the truth. It made me feel better about what I was doing if I was forthright about it. As long as I was being honest with him, then it made me not feel so badly. So here I was again. The decision made. It was for the best. He was such a sweet, caring man and I could not hurt him. The longer I pursued this relationship, the more he would end up hurt in the end. That's it! It's over. I am finished. I have to be! "We can remain friends," I said. He agreed. Bruce wanted to be my friend.

I can't even begin to tell you when we went from being "friends" to being "more than friends" again. It just happened. Something (maybe angels) kept me drawn to Familyman333. The courtship continued. The phone calls never stopped. The texts continued daily. Until...

Road Trip – Nashville Bound

It was a beautiful Tuesday evening, a kid-free night and Familyman333 asked me to come to Nashville. We would have dinner and I could spend the night and drive home the next day. Why not? I thought. He understands me. We understand each other. I have been honest with him about my intentions. So, why not go? I could not wait for the end of the work day to arrive. And I jumped in my red camaro and headed to Nashville, Tennessee!

When I pulled into his driveway, he was waiting on the porch, a buttery nipple in hand. He handed it to me and I took a sip, expressing the deliciousness of the drink with my "yums" and "mmmmm's", recalling the first time we shared that drink together. Then, he gave me a sensual, long kiss indicating his true gratefulness in seeing me. We walked into his home and he gave me the grand tour. He had purchased a "fixer upper" house in which he had begun some of the work, but he had a vision regarding the rest of the home. So he eloquently gave me his vision in words.

As we walked into the master bedroom, I saw the most beautiful king-sized bed. It was an antique white set decorated with a silk comforter and a multitude of pillows. Familyman333 had his man-cave and he was proud to show it to me. "Okay. Okay. I have to ask!" I exclaimed with the usual shrill in my voice that I get when I am excited. "You must tell me. Did the comforter on this bed belong to someone famous?" As Bruce revealed to me who the comforter belonged to, I gasped with excitement! Bruce replied, "Just Breathe, Sandy! Just Breathe!" Wow! Really! What a thought! Later that evening I would be crawling into the "Just Breathe" bed with my man. My Familyman333.

Song Application - "Just Breathe" – Faith Hill©

But first, we must take a tour of his infamous dry-cleaning shop, the shop that becomes home to the clothing of the stars and other distinguished people. We drove to the shop and began to walk through as Bruce explained the layout of the building. I was overwhelmed! This place was huge! I had no preconceived vision of what I would see when I walked into this building. But it was unbelievable! I became a teenager again. I had the giddy laugh, along with a mischievous, fun-loving, care-free attitude. I was having fun and it showed in my laughter and in my suggestive words.

"Okay, Mr. Willis," I said as I looked at him with a wink, "Does any of this clothing belong to someone important, that I can try it on and model for you, and you can slowly undress me, and we can know when it is delivered to their home that we have already christened it? When we see them wear it on stage, you will know it looked better on me… and off me?! MMMMM…..Well?" I laughed. He looked at me and smiled, as I ran from one piece of clothing to the next and said, "This one? Or.... this one?.....Or….. this one?"

Being in that building with Bruce Willis was like being in an amusement park, wondering what ride I could ride next. It was fun and it was exciting! Watching the excitement on his face as I teased him with the potential of this idea made me feel like a kid again. I could see the inquisitiveness in his eyes as he wondered what it would be like to actually fulfill this fantasy.

We made our way into the back room where various pieces of clothing were hanging on racks. As we walked through and he explained where some of the pieces came from, I spotted a robe, a god-awful ugly robe. My eyes immediately reflected what my brain thought. "Mr. Willis, my family man, are you thinking what I'm thinking?" I said with a smile. I made my way toward the robe motioning my index finger for him to follow. With the excitement of the clothing fantasy previously laid out before him, the longing and the desire were present. I took the robe off the rack and draped it over my shoulders as I motioned my Familyman333 to join me. Mr. Willis, being the business-conscious, thoughtful, and perceptive man that he is, knew that he wouldn't want to wear a piece of clothing that someone else had previously (intimately) worn. He immediately conveyed that this fantasy would have to wait for the "Just Breathe" bed.

We had planned to go to downtown Nashville that evening and listen to some music, but after the heated excitement of the shop tour, we decided to return home to the "Just Breathe" bed instead. Climbing into that bed was everything I thought it would be. Bruce was so overcome by passion and desire, and so was I. As we lay there in the warmth and comfort of each others' arms, I looked at him and exclaimed, "OMG, I really love the Just Breathe Bed!"

Bruce told me over and over how much fun I was, how sexy I was, and how much he enjoyed being with me. He revealed to me that he had felt things with me that he had never felt before. He truly enjoyed the way my body responded to his touch. This was amazing to him. "Just let me love you," he said. "Rule number 2."

Rule number 1: Whatever Sandy Wants

Rule number 2: Just Let Me Love You

"Wow!" I said. "I like these rules. I don't have to do anything. This is easy." Later, there would be two more rules added…

Rule number 3: I am important…I matter.

Rule number 4: Always remember the rules…that's all you have to do.

The Angel House

I hate admitting that throughout the beginning of my relationship/friendship with Mr. Familyman333, I didn't believe that he was my hole-in-one. I continued fishing. I continued catching fish. And I continued to throw them back. I kept looking for that perfect person for me, but something would not allow me to let Familyman333 go. Something kept pulling me back to this man. We talked daily. We continued to visit and hang out with each other. We had a lot fun. All the while, I was honest with him, telling him I didn't see a long-term relationship with him. Something was missing.

I explained to Bruce that I believed it had to do with my father issues. My father had sexually molested me when I was a young adult and then he died. He left this earth, unexpectedly, dying from a heart attack. I didn't get in a hurry to get to the hospital that day, and he passed away without seeing me. I have wondered often if my father would have made amends with me if he had been given the chance. This, I will never know.

I also had that mindset that I was still in my 20's and Mr. Willis was 59. I felt like he looked older than me and that everyone else thought that too. There was one time that I was talking with Belinda about this. I received an email from her that read:

> *"There is no Mr. Perfect. You are right. You ARE spending a lifetime looking for something that doesn't exist.*
>
> *Vain/Vanity - 1.Having or showing an excessively high opinion of one's appearance, abilities, or worth.*
>
> *Maybe you feel like you are "worth" more with someone that is perfect; but really what you are looking for is because of your fear of who you are.*
>
> *Look deep within yourself. Are you worried about how you feel/think or what others will think?*
>
> *Good men are hard to find. Love happens. Hatred happens. You have to love yourself first."*

Wow, she was right! I knew this. But, my mind continued to argue with my heart. I continued to shop online and I discovered the Magic Mirror Man (You read his story in a previous chapter). After meeting the Magic Mirror Man, I just could not follow him home that night. I had to go see my Familyman333. I felt like I was cheating on him and that just wasn't right. I could not make myself go home with this other man.

The evening that I met the Magic Mirror Man, I sent Bruce a text that said, "Going out with friends…and then…" Bruce replied to that text, "I wish I were your …and then." So, after leaving the Magic Mirror Man, I picked up my telephone and called Bruce. I said, "How would you like to be my . . . and then? I am about twenty minutes from your house."

Bruce was excited about seeing me. Funny thing is…as I drove to his house, I thought to myself, there are so few men in this world that you could actually feel comfortable enough to pick up the telephone and call on a Friday night, twenty minutes from their house, and know it would be okay that you just dropped by to see them. But Bruce was that kind of man. He was the one you knew you could trust. You never had to worry that he might be with someone else, or that he would tell you that you couldn't come. Bruce was thrilled to hear from me and couldn't wait to see me. And, yes, he met me at the door with my buttery nipple in hand. And a beautiful, sensual, longing kiss.

I was glad to be at home in my "Just Breathe" bed. Relaxed. Safe. Away from the world outside. I was at peace in the arms of the man that loved me, and I knew this. I was glad to be where I was. It was where I was meant to be. I was at myself here and I was safe and free-speaking. I could laugh here. I could cry here. And my dear angel was always there to do both with me.

The next morning, after departing the comforts of the "Just Breathe" bed, I walked into the restroom and looked in the mirror. There was no doubt in my mind that I had to look just absolutely terrible. As I looked into the mirror, I was surprised! "Wow, Bruce!" I exclaimed. "Look at my hair! I have never seen my hair look so good!" And it was beautiful! My hair was bouncy and full of life! In my entire life, I had never seen my hair look this incredible. "Bruce," I said, "Do you think that you could do my hair every day? I want you to fix my hair exactly like this…exactly the way you fixed it last night…every night. I so love what you have done to my hair!" (Sorry FSM #9…But, I have never seen my hair look like that again! LOL).

Later that day, we met his son, Tony, for lunch. His son was such a sweet young man and I was thrilled to meet him. Sitting at lunch that day, I was granted the opportunity to share my "1111 and 333" story with Tony. I made sure that I prefaced my story many times with, "I am skeptical." I didn't want him to believe that I was crazy. After all, I said I am skeptical, but I will never be one to say that it could never happen. The sweetest part was sharing about how his Dad fit into the story. After all, it was these associated numbers that led me to meet Mr. Willis and to continue in this relationship, even though other things were holding me back. I finished the story by saying, "So you see, this is why I believe your Dad was sent to me by God to be my angel."

Tony never said much. I couldn't tell by his eyes if he thought I was crazy or not. I wanted him to like me; I wanted to be accepted into his Dad's life and family.

Tony began to explain to his Dad that he was looking for a secondary residence in town. He and his wife lived on his wife's family farm, and they both worked in town. They felt the necessity to have something in the City to reduce commuting time. With my daily commute, I could really relate to this need.

Bruce told Tony that he had a friend who had a house that she rented short term to visitors in Nashville, but he would check with her to see if she was interested in renting the home on a long-term basis. Tony asked if we could go see the house, so we headed toward the home.

We walked onto the front porch. I looked to the right of the front door and there it was again. The house number was "1111" and hanging from the numbers was a silver angel! I looked at Tony and motioned my eyes toward the numbers. "Tony...Bruce...Look." They looked at each other with disbelief and I smiled. "See, it happens all the time," I said. From that day forward, this house became known as "The

Angel House." And my reasons for meeting Familyman333 became more and more apparent each day.

Song Application – "I Believe There Are Angels Among Us" – Alabama©

That afternoon, we went to "the farm." This was when I would meet Bruce's two daughters and his son-in-law. (I haven't had an opportunity to meet his other son, yet. He lives in Florida, near his Mom). Bruce had told me on more than one occasion that the two daughters and I were a lot alike, in our outgoing personalities, and that we would be dangerous together. I couldn't wait to meet them and test that observation. Maybe, I would add a few more FSM's to my FSM family. Smiling again.

Going to the farm was fun. Relaxing. We got to see the grandmother's home and it reminded me of what it was like years ago when homes were simple. There had been a meal prepared that day for the workers and a sheet had been draped across the bowls with the remaining food inside... the way people did it in the good old days, so that the food would be waiting for the next "neighbor" or farm hand that dropped by. There was always plenty of food no matter how many showed up. I felt like I was in my "Walton's" era.

We chatted a while and I met Jack. Bruce had helped him find a job when no-one else would help him. I can see what Bruce saw in this young man's heart. His smile lit up a room. He beamed from the inside out. His charisma would make anyone feel happy, even at the saddest of times. Yes, Jack was a person everyone wanted to be around. And Familyman333 put confidence in this young man when no-one else would believe in him or his abilities. This was one of the stories Bruce had shared with me earlier, so I was pleased to meet Jack and felt honored to make his presence.

Leaving the farm that day, I felt I had a new sense of who Bruce Willis, the Family Man really was. I already knew his character. That was revealed early in our relationship. But now I got to see Bruce as a father and he fulfilled the role very beautifully. I was proud to be with Bruce Willis that weekend, and knew I had made the right choice to drive to his house on Friday instead of going home with the Magic Mirror Man.

That evening I settled into the "Just Breathe" bed with my Familyman333. It had been a great weekend. We collapsed pretty early that evening, exhausted from the activities of the day and the evening before.

I hadn't been asleep long when I was awakened by a bright blue light outside the bedroom window. I peeked out the window and saw a police car parked right in front of Bruce's house. I woke Bruce up and he made his way to the front door to look outside and see if he could determine what was happening. I commented, "Bruce, close the door. This looks like a scene from a movie with the JAWS music playing in the background, and someone has escaped and is running through the neighborhood. He might see your open door and run inside and take us both hostage." We both laughed and made our way back to the safety of the "Just Breathe" bed.

For the first time, I wasn't able to breathe in the "Just Breathe" bed. I lay there looking out the window searching for the police. I could not see anyone. Hours passed. Bruce was sleeping like a baby, as I lay there questioning everything in my mind. "Who is this man? I don't really know him. We haven't really been together that long. All I know is what is in his profile and what he has elected to reveal to me. What if he is a thief? An ax-murderer!? What am I thinking? What am I doing?"

"How many times have you thought you knew someone to find out they weren't the person that you thought they were? How many times do you allow your heart to be so trusting only to be deceived again?" My mind went wild as I lay in the bed wondering if the police car would ever leave. It finally left, but only briefly. Then it returned again. I couldn't believe that Familyman333 was still asleep. This hadn't fazed him at all!

He was happy and content in his "Just Breathe" bed while I lie awake wondering who the hell he was!

The police finally left. I couldn't wait until morning to head home, back to the safety and security of my woman-cave. Later that evening, Bruce called and explained that he had gotten the complete story about the reasons the police were present that evening. There were several police in the neighborhood on varying streets attempting to catch someone. We just happened to be in the middle of the area that they were searching. I couldn't believe that my mind became so dramatic. Anxiety overcame me. I was really safe, just as I thought. In my "Just Breathe" bed with my FamilyMan333.

The Beach Trip

It was a beautiful day. I had a one-week trip planned for Gulf Shores, Alabama in which I had training and a meeting scheduled. My FSM's were joining me at the end of the week, but from Sunday until Wednesday, I would be alone. I decided to invite my Familyman333 to join me. And he anxiously accepted. This would give us time to be alone and at the beach. This would be a great few days in paradise.

The drive down was fun. We drove separate vehicles because he would be leaving on Wednesday. So, I followed him. We talked on our telephones almost the entire way. This was a great road trip, filled with anticipation of the time together. As we turned onto Gulf Shores Parkway, we stopped to get fuel. I went inside the store and returned to find Mr. Willis cleaning the ladies' windows in the parking lot. I walked up to him, smiled and said, "I can't take you anywhere without you flirting with all the beautiful ladies." The elder ladies in the car smiled and thanked him graciously. Bruce shared with me that while he was cleaning the windows of the camaro, a young man walked up and commented that he liked his car. Bruce responded, "This is my baby's car."

There it was! The vision in my head once again. "Bruce, do you realize what he thought? He thought that you were my sugar daddy!" I said. We laughed! Bruce always laughed with me. He realized the conflict that I was having with myself. He never got upset over this. He just continued being patient with me. He was never mean or frustrated. He showed such care for me. A simple man, with a lot of love to give.

We stopped on the way to the hotel and picked up a few things, including the ingredients for making our buttery nipples. After all, it was our celebratory drink! We must have these at the beach. Once we arrived to our room, we fixed a drink and walked out to the balcony to appreciate the view. It was fabulous! I recall kissing Bruce on the balcony and being glad to be at my favorite place with my Familyman333.

Bruce's patience is exemplary. I recall standing on the balcony and beginning to reposition the chairs so that we could sit and enjoy our view. There was a small table and I suggested that we put the table between the two chairs so that we would have a place to set our drinks. Bruce moved the table between the two chairs and we both sat down.

I looked over at him so far away, with the table between us and commented, "I don't like it. I can't hold your hand. Why don't we put the table back on the other side of your chair and move the two chairs closer together and I can set my drink on the big table on this side of me?" He smiled. Then he began obediently moving the table and chairs around just as I asked. As we both sat next to each other and joined hands, he smiled. "You knew this. This is what you were going to do anyway," I said. Bruce just smiled. He never said, "I told you so!" He never called me names or told me how stupid I was (which is what I had been accustomed to in an earlier relationship). He just smiled. "Why didn't you just tell me?" I asked. His reply, as humble as it could be, "We got the same result accomplished, didn't we? I knew you would figure it out!"

Wow, this man is so different from anyone I have ever met. Non-confrontational! Just a genuine heart the size of Texas and he gives a piece of it to everyone he meets! This man is truly incredible!

I must say that a trip to the beach with a loving, caring man could not go without a little passion. We purchased strawberries and whipped cream at the store and after a few drinks decided a little play time was warranted. We made our way into the bedroom. It wasn't the "Just Breathe" bed, but we were at the beach. I am sure the exchange would have to work. Smiling. Of course it would work. I was with my Familyman333 and we had buttery nipples and strawberries and whipped cream! Life was definitely good.

Being with Bruce in Gulf Shores, away from family, alone, with the romance of the sound of the waves in the background, paved a new way for us. "I want to retire at the beach," I said. Bruce smiled and agreed. "Rule #1 – Whatever Sandy Wants."

The frolic and fun of being with Bruce was always rampant. We laughed about so many things. I had shared with Bruce about my digestive (stomach) issues and he was aware so when my stomach began to hurt from the great food and drinks, Bruce began to give me a colon massage! Yes, I know, this isn't very romantic as compared to flowers or the strawberries and whipped cream, or the sunset on the balcony. But this is life. Lying next to someone you are comfortable with and asking them to give you a colon massage is life…and FUNNY! As he is massaging my tummy (my colon), he said to me, "Do I **MOVE** you, baby?" I erratically lost it! Literally! I thought I would pee my pants. I laughed so hard. I had to get up and leave the bed as I laughed until I cried! My Familyman333 truly makes me happy!

As I said, I was in Gulf Shores for a meeting, so I had to get out of bed the next morning to attend class. I came back to the room at lunch break, and Bruce had placed roses in the room. He placed six roses each on the night stand and on the bathroom vanity. He then spread the rose petals along the floor and the counter near the roses. It was such a sweet romantic gesture. And he wasn't around for me to thank. He had taken my car into town and detailed it so that I would have a clean car to drive the rest of the week. He is such a kind, considerate, loving man.

Three nights in Gulf Shores with my Familyman333 was a very romantic and carefree time. There came the morning that he would leave. I was saddened by his departure, but somehow knew that this was the last time that I would see him. My mind had continued the battle with my heart and I just could not continue leading him on. Yes, I loved what I felt while with this man. I loved the romance. I loved his genuine heart. But he was still OLD! Damn!

FORE

It had been two weeks since the beach trip. I began to drift away from Familyman333. I knew that I could not keep leading him on the way that I was doing. I was being selfish by staying in his life. I was selfish because I wasn't there for Bruce. Instead I was in his life for me…for the way he made me feel. I enjoyed my safety net and appreciated the comfort that I felt when in his arms and in the "Just Breathe" bed. This was wrong! I just couldn't hurt him by continuing to stay.

205

I never revealed any of this to Bruce. I just couldn't. Saying the words out loud to him would make it final and subconsciously, I didn't want finality with him. And if I said it, that would make it real. Then, it would hurt him; it would inevitably hurt him. I could not do that. So, I just said nothing. Nothing! The phone calls got less and less. The texts were almost non-existent. I was slowly drifting away from Familyman333. Until:

One evening (or should I say morning), around 2:30 a.m., I received a text from Familyman333, the text that could have changed his screen name to "broken-heartedman333." I could hear his broken heart in his words. "You can finish our chapter now Sandy, now that you know how it ends."

My heart dropped! My stomach was filled with butterflies! The realization behind the words touched my heart with overwhelming heart-break and pain! I could not lose my Familyman333. It was at this moment, tears began to endlessly flow! It was as if all emotion inside of me was released. Revealed to my mind, very abruptly by my heart, at this moment I realized that I had fallen in love with Familyman333 and I had to tell him!

"I love you, Mr. Bruce Willis, and I love the way you love me, with everything you have. You make it so easy to love you back." I said. His reply was, "Thank you for choosing to love me. There is so much that I want to learn about you…we have many laughter-filled moments ahead…"

I thought to myself, he is wrong. I never **chose** to love him. So, I replied back to him, "Hey, babe, let me break it down for you. I did not CHOOSE to love you. As a matter of fact, I think I fought it with everything in me. My heart chose you. I have been on a quest to find what my mind told me that I was looking for…but my heart decided differently." Bruce's answer…as honest as he is…knowing my mind… " LOL, Let's hope your mind stays on board!!" I have been at this place in our relationship with Bruce so many times that I am sure he doubts me. But he says, "ROFL...I will love you as long as you will let me, Sandy. MUUAAAAAH!"

Familyman333 is such a good man. He is the epitome of the inherent goodness of man. I responded to his text as sincerely as I could, "Awwww, baby, I don't ever want to hurt you again. I hope that this is forever. Can you handle forever?" Bruce's most heartfelt response, "I know that what you say is true. I love unconditionally, totally, with no concerns about how long it will last. We have no promise for anything but today, so I simply hope for a lifetime of todays." (Wow! This sounds like a Hallmark Card....maybe I should place the copywrite sign here right now...LOL!©).

Is it possible? Can this man...ANY man truly love me this much? How will my story end? Have I found my Mr. Right? Is it "Familyman333?" If so, this chapter of my life has come to an end. I have found the man of my dreams, my Familyman333. There is no doubt that the angels and God brought him to me, and there is no doubt that God and the angels are keeping me with him. Everything about him tells me that he is my angel, from the November 11 birthday to the Angel House; he is truly my Familyman333. I know he was sent to protect me; to make me feel safe, and to finally be the man in my life that loves me unconditionally, the way that I deserve. I thank God daily for Mr. Bruce Willis. Bamagirlluvsu has been laid to rest out in cyber land, but she is alive and well here in the REAL world, loving her Familyman333 with all her heart!

♥ ♥Mr. Right♥ ♥

Is Familyman333 my true love, or is it possible that I may never find my soul mate because my heart is always open to love? My heart is filled with tenderness and I can truly love almost anyone. This book was not meant to be about my father issues, but I guess it could be. My heart is open. I can love unconditionally with all that I have. I can forgive. I can forget. And I can love again. It is what my father taught me.

My heart knows the difference now. I don't have to accept the way men choose to treat me. What my father did was wrong. When men choose to mistreat or disrespect women, it is because of something they are missing in their own hearts. It has nothing to do with the women that they hurt.

Will my heart continue to argue with my mind to protect itself? Absolutely! My heart now knows that it is okay to be occupied with unconditional love, but those conditions are limited to what is right. No woman or man should ever accept less than real honor, loyalty, and respect. Anything else is not real love at all.

Maybe, I have spent enough time cyber dating. This started as an adventure. It was a lot of fun. I met many interesting people. Made some friends. And made some enemies. A lot of lessons learned. One lesson was this. We may sit behind the computer and we may represent ourselves as being happy, strong, and independent. We may give the grand appearance of being successful and confident in whom we are, but behind each of our on-line profiles is a real person…a human being. We all have a story. We have all been through pain and suffering. We hurt. We cry. And we all long for that comfort zone…the "Just Breathe" bed.

The biggest lesson learned. I developed a mentality that "so what if it doesn't work out with this guy…or this one…there is always one more…" Plenty of Fish©. Yes. There truly are a lot of available dates out there. The general rule…which stands to reason…they would either love me or they would hate me. There is no in between. I got my feelings hurt…my pride stepped upon many times. After all, I AM BAMAGIRLLUVSU! I am who I am in the profile and so much more! I believed in myself and I believed in love.

I made many road trips to find my soul mate, my partner, my friend. And I came home many times let down and disappointed. Yes, I had expectations. I had THE list…not the written one, but the mental one. I had to have this list. Without it, I might be meeting my next ex-husband. I NEVER wanted to go through that again. So, I developed the mentality after my rejections, "So what? I will just get back online and shop some more. There is always one more where that one came from." And I would search until I found one more potential date.

Inter-twined in these meetings of rejection were also those that I rejected. The people that I hurt. And I am not the person that can hurt others easily. It was hard for me. I didn't want to let go. There were so many times that I would meet someone and know that it wasn't right, but this person would be so into me, and would treat me so respectfully, with honor or care. I was like a sponge, soaking it all in. When you have lived through the life that I have lived through…the search…the quest…became the goal or drive to feel good again. To regain my own self-respect…my own honor. After all, I am worthy and deserving. (Rule #3).

There were definitely many lessons learned. Honestly, I really didn't recognize the biggest lessons until I began to put my adventures into words. Bamagirlluvsu, the adventures and the book, became a form of cyber-psycho analysis. Bamagirlluvsu provided an opportunity to learn and grow.

I believed in the fairness of the world with "Scott, the Entertainer."

I learned to believe in ME again with "My Journey with Bernie."

I cried and remembered what it felt like to think you were dying with the "Cross Country Lover."

I relived my childhood with the "Birmingham Photographer."

I got to spend one more day with my Mom with "the Canada man."

I learned that there is still distrust in the world with "the Hockey Scout" and "that damn bridge to South Africa."

I learned to dance again, with joy and passion, and to appreciate life's luxuries and "bucket list" items with "the Baby Daddy."

I re-learned to live your life like you are dying from my reunion with the "Blast from the Past."

I learned that I can be WRONG with Engineer4, as I later discovered first impressions aren't always right.

I learned about the dangers of modern day technology with "the school teacher."

I learned that there are still some jerks in the world with "dirtbikerider" (who didn't know that?).

I learned that even though "Jackson" and "the Father of the Year" didn't believe I was worthy, I still was.

I learned that life is sad for people like "the Magic Mirror Man" and "Black Jack Player" as they spend their entire lives working and not knowing how to love and live…

I learned that you can invest more than money with Mr. "Invest in Me" and still be a winner.

AND…

I learned to believe in angels and the goodness of man again with "Familyman333."

I learned a little more about love and life with all of the men that came into my life the last two years. I don't know exactly what will happen to Bamagirlluvsu. I only know that life is too short and I won't give up…on myself…or on the inherent goodness of men. God gave us the ability to open our hearts and love. To forgive. And love again.

My wish for you is that this book may somehow change your life! That the stories of romance and adventure will touch each of you in some way, that you are able to take your own life's experiences and get out there…and touch someone else's life. We all come into each others' lives for a reason. And you will never know whose life or heart you can touch unless you take a chance.

The Song Application above all other song applications - "I Hope You DANCE!" – Lee Ann Womack©

JUST DANCE!

Sandy Gowers

www.ingramcontent.com/pod-product-compliance
Lightning Source LLC
Chambersburg PA
CBHW071147050326
40689CB00011B/2011